THE KING'S ARMY

THE KING'S ARMY

Copyright © 2022 by Jake Uniacke

All rights reserved. This book or any portion thereof may not be reproduced or used in any manner whatsoever without the express written permission of the publisher except for the use of brief quotations in a book review.

This is a work of fiction. Names, characters, places, and incidents either are the product of the author's imagination or are used fictitiously. Any resemblance to actual persons, living or dead, events, or locales is entirely coincidental.

Cover design by Stone Ridge Books

Paperback ISBN-13: 9798423185572
Hardcover ISBN-13: 9798423186494

@author_jakeu
www.authorjakeu.wordpress.com

THE KING'S ARMY

JAKE UNIACKE

Also by Jake Uniacke:
Lighthouse
The Girl from Under the Water

I

SPLASH.

He sat by the river's edge, tossing stones into the water, watching them skid across the surface before they dropped to the bottom. A smile stretched across Caleb's face as he admired his stone tossing skills. It was the only talent he really had. Everyone else in the Shihan Kingdom had some form of magic. But not Caleb. He was different. Born without magic, Caleb had struggled throughout his entire life. The Khrishan War began three years ago, ending just six months ago, and whilst all the male elves in the kingdom were able to battle, Caleb had to stay in the safety of his own home. He couldn't protect his father either—he was killed in battle, leaving his wife a single mother to Caleb and Jasmine.

Caleb watched the world go by—dragons circulated in the air above him, while clouds floated through the sky, travelling from one end to the other. It was a sunny day in the Shihan Kingdom and Caleb wanted to just have a peaceful day for a change. Every day, something always happens, and Caleb had quite frankly had enough of it. Today, he would relax.

The young elf threw another stone into the river, watching it skid across the water's surface. Again, he

THE KING'S ARMY

smiled. Suddenly, a voice boomed from behind him, calling his name hysterically.

"Caleb!" the voice yelled. "Caleb!"

Caleb turned around, muttering "Oh shit, here we go," and watched the village Messenger race toward him, trying to catch his breath. The Messenger stopped in front of the elf and pulled a scroll from his belt.

"The King summons all elves to the Garden of Kate. He has an urgent message for everyone," the Messenger read.

"What's this message about?" asked Caleb.

"King Bartholomew will reveal all in due course. You need to get to the Garden of Kate as soon as possible. His Highness won't be best pleased if you're late."

The Messenger headed East, obviously to hassle some other innocent elves just minding their own business. Caleb stood up and headed back through the forest. The leaves crunched beneath his dirty sandals, disturbing the insects crawling around in the mud. Caleb trudged past the trees that towered over him, watching his every move. At the end, he saw a light. The end of the forest.

The young elf hurried his pace, hoping to get to the end of the forest so he could get this over and done with. He hated when the king had an announcement. It was always something negative such as someone being given a death sentence or someone in the royal family had been killed. Caleb hoped this time it would be something positive, but he wasn't going to hold his breath over it.

THE KING'S ARMY

Caleb exited the forest and headed along the gravel path, the uneven surface causing him to wobble. The Garden of Kate was visible in the distance and a large crowd of elves had already made their way there. The king's stand was positioned by the entrance of the garden. He wasn't there yet. But Caleb could see him making his way down on his dragon as it swooped through the sky.

Caleb hurried his pace again to ensure he wasn't punished by His Highness for being late. He pushed his way through the crowd to find his mother and sister who were waiting by the fountain at the centre of the garden. His mother, Meredith, was holding the handles of Jasmine's wheelchair, ensuring she couldn't roll away. Caleb approached them and gave his sister a kiss on the forehead before hugging his mother.

"You took your time," said Meredith. "Where have you been?"

"I was at the river," Caleb said.

The family of three stopped talking as everyone else fell silent, watching the guards in the distance take their positions.

"Citizens of Shihan," a voice boomed. "Please bow for His Highness, King Bartholomew!"

All the elves in the garden knelt on one knee and bowed their heads as King Bartholomew made his grand entrance. His dragon dived towards the crowd, but they weren't allowed to move. Caleb watched out of the corner of his eye as the dragon came to a stop and

THE KING'S ARMY

the king climbed down, making his way over to his stand.

"You may all stand," said King Bartholomew. His big, bushy beard hung to his stomach, golden chains hanging around his neck. His face was wrinkled with age yet didn't look a day close to dying. Considering he was almost in his hundreds, the king was extremely healthy.

Everyone stood up again and stood politely as the king took his position at his stand. He cleared his throat.

"I'm afraid I have some bad news," he said.

Caleb rolled his eyes. *I knew it.*

"My daughter has been kidnapped."

All the elves began to mutter amongst themselves, shock and despair rushing through them. One mother even screamed, the sound of it haunting Caleb—was it really *that* bad?

"Quiet!" yelled the king. "As you may imagine, this is a very tough time for my family. Without our beautiful daughter, Princess Kate, we are not a united family. We can only hope for her safe return."

The king stopped speaking as once again, the residents of the Shihan Kingdom muttered to one another, conspiracy theories flying from one to the other. Caleb turned to his mother, worried about what the king might say next.

"Due to this awful incident," King Bartholomew continued, "I am going to need an army. I'll need an army of warriors to take on the voyage to the Ice

THE KING'S ARMY

Kingdom where we believe she may have been taken. I'm sure the Winter Queen has taken her. A terrible incident indeed. We are hosting registration for the King's Army at 7am tomorrow morning. I expect to see many of you there. That will be all."

King Bartholomew stepped down from his stand and galloped back over to his dragon, before it flew back into the air and headed North, where the king's palace was located. Caleb looked at his mother and sister.

"Don't even think about signing up, Caleb," said Jasmine. "You know you can't do it."

"I can do anything I put my mind to," Caleb protested. "If I want to sign up to the army, then I will. There's nothing about me that will lessen my chances."

"Except you don't have any magic! What happens if you need to use powers to fight against whatever is out there? You don't stand a chance of surviving."

"I have to try."

Meredith interrupted her son. "No, you don't. Your sister is right, you have no chance of surviving this. If you sign up for the army, I'll never forgive you. I lost your father in battle, I'm not going to lose you too."

❀

Caleb slouched in the wicker chair. He huffed. Meredith placed a mug of soup in front of him but didn't say

THE KING'S ARMY

a word. Instead, she just glared at him. Caleb took the mug from the table and sipped a small amount.

"I'm sorry, Mum," said Caleb.

"What for?" Meredith asked.

"I know you don't want me to enter the King's Army. But I really want to. I want to prove to everyone in the kingdom that I can do things like this. I know I'm not like everyone else. But I am just as worthy as they are."

Meredith folded a kitchen towel and flopped it over the drying rail. "I do understand. I really do. I'm just scared for you. You could be trained on all the weapons in the world and still get killed because you have no magic."

"What if I ask for the king's blessing?" Caleb suggested. "I could ask him if he can bless me with a power, even if it is just a small one."

Meredith laughed. "It doesn't work like that, honey. The king doesn't just bless anyone who asks him. They must prove themselves for his blessing."

"That's exactly why I need to enter his army. I prove myself; he blesses me with magic. Simple."

Meredith shook her head and grabbed her son's hand, holding it tight. "Listen to me. You are not entering the King's Army. Like I said before, I'm not losing you too."

Jasmine came into the room and smiled at Caleb. She wheeled her chair next to him and took hold of his hand. "Are you entering the King's Army?"

THE KING'S ARMY

"I guess not," Caleb grumbled petulantly. "Mum said I'm not allowed, so I guess I'm not going to enter. Even as a fully grown man, I'm still not allowed to make my own choices."

"Don't take that tone against me," snapped Meredith. "You might be twenty-two, but you're still my baby and I'm still going to do everything to protect you. If that means locking you in this house, then I will!"

"That's a breach of my rights," joked Caleb. "I've already said I'm not going to enter; you have my word."

Caleb stood up and grabbed his cloak, hooking it around his shoulders. Meredith stopped him at the door.

"Where are you going?" she asked.

"I'm going to see Shayne," said Caleb. "Is that okay?"

"Fine. Don't let him drag you into anything."

"I won't."

Caleb swung the door open and slammed it shut behind him. He hurried through the village, dirt gathering between his toes. The resident elves went about their daily business, some pulling carts of bread while others sharpened their weapons. Caleb could spot them glaring at him out the corner of his eye. Everyone knew about his disability, and many had always judged him for it—particularly the men.

Shayne stood in the distance under the doorway to the bakery. He waved to Caleb and they both moved towards each other.

"Who's put a bee in your bonnet?" Shayne said.

THE KING'S ARMY

Caleb tried to hide his grouchy face, but it was an impossible task. "My mum. She's banning me from entering the King's Army."

"Seriously? Caleb, you're a fully grown adult. She can't ban you from doing anything."

"Are you entering?"

Shayne went silent for a few seconds before answering. "I'm thinking about it. Do you want to enter?"

Caleb nodded. "I want to. I really want to prove to everyone that I'm capable. But I know my mum will hate me. She lost my father in battle, what if she loses me too?"

Shayne placed a hand on Caleb's shoulder and looked at him directly in the eyes. "You can't think like that. Princess Kate is in danger; she needs our help. Enter the army, don't enter the army. It's your choice —just make sure you make the *right* choice."

"I guess you're right," said Caleb. "Are you definitely entering? I could really do with a friend in there."

"I will if you will."

Caleb nodded and held his hand out for a handshake. Shayne took it and they shook hands for a brief moment.

"Deal," they both said.

2

THE SUN SHONE through Caleb's window, waking him up. He grunted as he stretched across his bed, getting his bones and muscles ready for the day. Today, he would betray his mother's wishes. Registration for the King's Army was today, and Caleb knew he was about to enter one of the most dangerous battles he had ever witnessed. Saving the king's daughter was going to be a dangerous and difficult mission. But it was something he wanted to do. It was something he *needed* to do.

Caleb sneaked out of the house and rushed along the pathway into the village. It would take him a while to get to the palace, but he didn't mind. His mother wouldn't wake for another hour or so yet, so Caleb knew he had plenty of time to get to the palace before his mother found him and dragged him back home.

"Caleb!" a voice yelled.

Caleb spun around and wobbled backwards as Shayne dashed towards him, swinging his arms around his torso.

"Get off!" Caleb spat.

Shayne let go and jumped around, giddy like a child. "You didn't change your mind then?"

"Why would I change my mind? I said this is something I want to do and I'm going to do it."

THE KING'S ARMY

"Are you one hundred percent sure you want to do this? Mummy will be very angry with you."

Caleb shook Shayne's sarcastic comment off and wandered out of the village and up a steep hill, taking him through a country road. Shayne hurried after him.

"Do you think the king will even let you join the army?" Shayne asked.

"Why wouldn't he?" Caleb said.

"Well, you don't have any magic. You're not like the rest of us."

Caleb rolled his eyes. "Thanks for the reminder."

"I just mean that His Highness might not see you as fit and worthy of being part of his army. He needs strong men."

Caleb stopped and looked his friend up and down, giggling at his slim figure which didn't have an ounce of muscle on it. "And you're a strong man, are you?"

Shayne fell silent and didn't respond to Caleb's comment. Instead, he wandered ahead of Caleb. Caleb walked after him and they didn't speak for a while.

"If the king doesn't let me join the army because of my disability," said Caleb, "then that just shows the kind of man he is. He cannot discriminate against me."

"I know what you mean," Shayne said. "But you can't get your hopes up. You know what the king is like. He's a dick!"

"I know that. But still, it's worth a try, isn't it?"

Shayne shrugged. "I suppose."

THE KING'S ARMY

The two friends reached the stairway that led to the palace. They both looked up and wondered how long it would take them to reach the top. It went on for miles into the clouds.

"We'll never make it up there," said Shayne.

"We're going to have to," Caleb replied. "If we want to prove to the king that we're worthy of being in his army, the least we can do is climb a staircase."

Shayne huffed and led the way up the stairs. The uneven surface caused the two friends to wobble but luckily, they managed to keep themselves upright.

Caleb looked back and saw his village disappear further and further into the distance as he climbed higher up the stairway. Shayne slipped and fell backwards. Caleb attempted to catch him, but he couldn't get a grip on Shayne's body, and he watched his friend tumble down the stairs. Moments later, Shayne floated back into the air and landed behind Caleb.

"I forgot about my powers," Shayne said with a laugh. "Just imagine, if you fell down then you'd be dead."

"Can you just shut up for five minutes about my lack of powers?" snapped Caleb. "I'm getting sick of it!"

Shayne surrendered and continued up the stairs, following Caleb to the top. A large gate was open at the top with a mile long queue of elves outside. Each one looked the same to Caleb - bushy beards, hairy chests, muscles the size of mountains. Caleb began to regret his decision of joining the army, but it was too late. It wasn't even certain he would be allowed in anyway.

THE KING'S ARMY

The palace staff had to assess every elf that registered, and the king would make the final decision. Caleb knew nothing about what the army would entail. The king didn't make it very clear yesterday. All he knew was this was something he had to do. He needed to prove to everyone he loved and everyone in the Shihan Kingdom that he *could* do it.

Caleb and Shayne joined the end of the queue and waited for their turn to enter the registration rink. The elf in front of Caleb turned around and let out a booming laugh.

"You two will never get in," he said. "Look at you, pair of idiots."

"Get stuffed," Caleb hissed.

The elf turned back around and giggled to himself. Caleb wanted to attack. But he knew he wouldn't win. Not yet anyway. The elf in front's muscular build formed a shadow across Caleb's body, blocking the light from his view.

Slowly, the queue into the registration rink became shorter and Caleb was almost at the front.

"Are you nervous?" Shayne asked.

"No," said Caleb, "what makes you think that?"

"Your legs are wobbling for a start."

Caleb looked down and watched his knees wobble like an earthquake was rushing through his body. He moved further forward and the gates to the palace were directly in front of him. He was up next. A guard approached him and grabbed his arm, pulling him through the gates and over to the registration tent. A lady with a short haircut and a butch body stood in front of him but didn't make eye contact. Instead, she just stared at the scroll in front of her.

"Name?" she asked.

"Caleb."

The lady wrote Caleb's name on the scroll and asked him for other details such as his height, age, hair colour, weight. and body type. She didn't look at him. Not once. She ushered Caleb on his way, and he was soon greeted by another member of the palace staff.

"Hello," Caleb replied. "I'm not sure exactly what's—"

"Sit down and be quiet."

The man pointed to a wooden chair at the edge of the rink where Caleb went to sit. His best friend approached him a moment later and sat in the empty chair.

"That woman at the entrance was a grumpy bitch, wasn't she?" giggled Shayne. "Seen more enthusiasm on a goat being slaughtered!"

"They're all grumpy in here," muttered Caleb. "One of the staff didn't say a word to me except when he told me to sit down and shut up."

Shayne giggled.

"It's not funny."

The two men sat in their chairs silently. Caleb looked up and watched as baby dragons flew through the clouds, small blazes of fire escaping their mouths. The sun shone into his eyes, making him squint. He

THE KING'S ARMY

looked in a completely different direction when he heard the royal fanfare play.

"Can everyone who has already registered please make their way to the Fitting Tent, where you'll be measured up for your battle gear," the Messenger announced over a megaphone.

Caleb wandered over to the Fitting Tent, following a crowd of larger elves. His mind buzzed with emotions and thoughts. The feeling of guilt bubbled within him, and the thought of failure made his stomach swim. Knowing he had just betrayed his mother and his sister, and knowing he could get killed, made Caleb want to pull out. But he *needed* to do this.

⊂⋌⊃

The tent smelled like dirt and damp. Caleb gagged as he sat down in a chair next to the smelliest part of the tent. It had the stench of piss. A palace tailor entered the tent and called each elf up one by one and made them stand in front of him, as still as possible, whilst he measured them from all angles.

Caleb's nerves increased as he knew it was almost his turn to go up. Everyone would laugh at him. He was the skinniest of the bunch. Although he had some muscles to show, he wasn't nearly as well built as the others. Like always, he would be the joke of the kingdom.

"Caleb?" the tailor called.

THE KING'S ARMY

Everyone turned to look at him. They all knew who he was. Caleb looked around, everyone watching him like a hawk.

"Caleb?!" the tailor called again, a little angrier this time.

Caleb jumped back in his seat, startled by the tailor's tone. He stood up and trudged over to the centre of the tent.

"Arms up," said the tailor.

Caleb lifted his arms above his head. Roars of laughter sounded around him, his face turning a shade of tomato red.

"Out to the side you stupid twit!" snapped the tailor.

Caleb held his arms out to the sides and the tailor wrapped a tape measure around his waist, noting down measurements in brief intervals.

"Stand straight."

Caleb put his arms down and stood as straight and as still as he possibly could. Again, the tailor got his tape measure out and measured Caleb's height. Caleb hadn't been paying much attention to the other elves having their measurements taken so he wasn't sure what to expect. When the tailor was finished, he ushered Caleb back to his seat and called up the next elf.

"He's a bit of a dick," Caleb whispered.

"They're all dicks in this palace," said Shayne. "Apparently, it's because the royals treat them like crap. It's understandable, I guess."

THE KING'S ARMY

Caleb shrugged. "Yeah, but no need to take it out on us."

Shayne mumbled and turned to watch the other elves get measured up.

※

A female tailor entered the tent, bubbly and giddy like a child. She sat her bag on an empty chair and stood in the centre, pushing the tailor to the side.

"Your uniforms are being measured," she said. "My name is Annabelle and I'm going to be your tailor from now on."

Annabelle shot a glare at the tailor. "Time for you to leave, Paul."

At least we finally know his name. He never introduced himself. Rude.

Caleb glared at Annabelle, lust in his eyes. He couldn't take his eyes off her. She was everything he wanted in a woman. He stared at her chest, and his eyes darted down to her backside. A hand slipped in front of his face, followed by the click of fingers. Caleb woke again.

"You want her, don't you?" Shayne giggled.

"No, course not. I'm in the army to save the princess and be with her. Not this lady," Caleb lied. "But my *God* she is stunning!" Caleb's gaze directed back to Annabelle.

"Right," shouted Annabelle. "You, come here." She pointed at Caleb.

THE KING'S ARMY

Caleb fell back off his chair, startled by Annabelle's sudden tone.

"I'm waiting."

"Sorry," Caleb grunted. "I'm fine, by the way."

Caleb scrambled off the floor and rubbed the back of his head, feeling the sharp stabbing pain shoot through his skull.

"Good. In that case, you can come up here and try on this uniform."

Caleb rolled his eyes and stood up, trudging over to Annabelle. He stood in front of her, awaiting her instructions. And as soon as she began giving him instructions, it didn't surprise him that they were exactly the same was the other tailor's instructions.

"Right," said Annabelle, "that's you done. Next."

Then, Caleb went back to his seat.

3

SILENCE.

The corridors within the palace were silent. Caleb looked around him, taking in his surroundings, mesmerised by the glamour that sat around him. He took a few steps forward and stopped in the centre of the palace ballroom. A candle chandelier hung above him, glowing in the tiny flames atop the candles. The walls at the top of the staircase were filled with portraits of past royalty.

Caleb felt a heavy shove against him, causing him to stumble and fall to the ground.

"Watch where you're standing!" Tobias hissed.

"You watch where you're going!" snapped Caleb.

Caleb stood up and lunged towards Tobias, striking him across the face. Tobias fought back, rubbing his hands together and pushing a wave of energy at Caleb. Caleb flew backwards, smashing through the staircase banister, before hitting the ground with a thud. Caleb grumbled, wincing as pain shot through his spine. Holding his back, Caleb struggled to his feet, the discomfort spreading through his entire body.

"That'll teach you," grumbled Tobias.

THE KING'S ARMY

Caleb watched as Tobias and the other elves walked off, chuckling to themselves. Shayne hurried over and helped keep his friend on his feet.

"Are you okay?" Shayne asked.

"Yeah, I'm fine," Caleb growled. "I *need* magic powers. How am I going to survive the King's Army?"

Shayne sighed. "You made the choice to sign up. You want to prove to everyone you can survive without magic. Stop with this negativity."

"I can't help it when things like this happen. I need to be able to fight properly."

"There are other ways to fight." Shayne placed a hand on Caleb's shoulder. "There's lots of weapons here. There could be someone to teach you how to use them."

Caleb walked in the direction of the other elves and Shayne quickly caught up. A large, golden door stood in front of everyone. It was closed and everyone was curious about what they were about to be greeted with. Nobody said a word.

The door clicked, startling everyone. It opened loudly, the creaking of the hinges echoing throughout the palace. As the door opened wide, Caleb's mouth dropped, saliva drooling from the side. A large table sat in the centre of the room, stretching from the far end all the way to the entrance. Across the table sat a large hog roast, plates with mountains of carrots, potatoes, parsnips, and many other vegetables, an array of plates with different meats on them, and lots of other sweet treats too.

THE KING'S ARMY

The army applicants entered the room and stood behind a chair each, as stated in the royal rules - when entering the palace dining hall, stand behind a chair and wait to be seated by the king. Caleb stood anxiously. What was the point of this meal? Was this the first task? Eat properly and you're in, eat like a savage and you're out?

King Bartholomew entered the dining hall and approached his throne at the far end of the table. He sat down first and placed both hands gently on the table.

"Please," he said, "be seated."

Everyone pulled their chairs from under the table and politely sat down, not daring to touch any of the food until the king had taken his first - unless he offered otherwise.

King Bartholomew took a sword and raised it in the air before slamming it down into the hog roast sat in the centre of the table. He cut through it and took large slices of the meat, slapping them onto his plate. He stuffed his grubby hands into the bowls of vegetables and dropped them onto his plate.

Caleb watched in disgust. Did this man not have *any* manners? He glanced over at Shayne who was turning his nose up at the food. Nobody knew where the king's hands had been and now, they were all over the food. Suddenly, Caleb wasn't hungry anymore.

"Tuck in," said the king.

Reluctantly, one of the elves made the first move and took a spoonful of potatoes before turning his attention to the hog roast. Small specs of dirt were dotted

THE KING'S ARMY

around the food, obviously fallen from the king's fingernails.

"Are you all shy?" King Bartholomew boomed. "I said tuck in!"

Caleb filled his plate with food and slowly ate his way through. He didn't want to appear rude so he made sure he took as much food as he could, even if he didn't manage to stomach all of it.

The meal was quiet, except for the odd burp and fart from the king. He had no table manners whatsoever. Caleb still didn't understand why he was having lunch with the king. He had no idea why *any* of the elves here were having lunch with the king when it wasn't even certain they were going to be in the army. But this was the biggest meal he had had in weeks, so he wasn't about to complain - except for the fact King Bartholomew had spread his dirty hands all over the food.

As soon as the meal ended, the elves made their way out of the dining hall and back into the ballroom where they were met by the Palace Guide. The Guide introduced himself as Omid, and he took the army applicants to the waiting room.

"Please take a seat," said Omid. "As soon as the king is ready for the meeting, his assistant will collect you."

Omid left the room. Caleb sat on an empty seat next to Shayne and looked out of the window to his left. The palace grounds were still swarmed with many men

THE KING'S ARMY

and women, some of whom Caleb assumed were signing up for the King's Army.

The door swung open, and a lady dressed in gold stood in the doorway. "His Highness is ready for you all now."

She allowed the men to leave the room and she took them to the courtroom where King Bartholomew was stood at his pew, ready and waiting for the elves to arrive. They each took a seat, and Caleb decided to sit towards the back with Shayne.

King Bartholomew cleared his throat. "Welcome to the Shihanian Palace. You are here because you've decided to apply for my army. Tonight, I will decide who the recruits will be, and they'll be announced tomorrow."

Caleb looked at the ground. He knew he didn't stand a chance against anyone else here.

The king continued his speech. "But I don't want to just read from a scroll about each of you. I want to get to know you in person. So, this meeting is all about getting to know each other. Strengths, weaknesses etcetera."

Caleb shivered. He knew as soon as the king saw him up close, that would be it. He'd be the joke of the room. No one would take him seriously. After all, no one took him seriously earlier in the tent anyway. He bounced his leg nervously. Shayne grabbed his leg to stop him bouncing it.

"Calm your nerves," Shayne whispered. "You'll be okay."

THE KING'S ARMY

King Bartholomew stood up and pointed to the first elf in the courtroom — Milo.

"Introduce yourself," the king boomed.

Milo stood up, arms behind his back. "My name is Milo. I'm twenty-four and being here is a dream come true."

The room fell silent, much to the king's dismay. "Continue."

Milo looked around, not knowing what to say. He tried to speak but no words came out. Caleb watched, knowing this would be him soon. Like Milo, Caleb was shy and never really knew the right words to say, especially in public situations.

"My biggest weakness is my shyness. But my biggest strength is fighting that," Milo said.

"Boring!" King Bartholomew snapped. "Next!"

Milo was pushed to his seat by Jesse who immediately took centre stage, wanting all the attention on him. Caleb scowled, giving an evil side-eye look to Jesse, the biggest bully here. He bit his tongue, stopping himself from raging at the king for the way he dismissed Milo like he was nothing.

"I'm Jesse. I have no weaknesses, I'm stronger than everyone here. My magic means I can teleport from one place to the other. I can't teleport far, but I can go far enough to win whatever fight I'm in," said Jesse, smugly.

"That sounds like a weakness to me," Caleb muttered.

"Who said that?"

THE KING'S ARMY

Caleb jumped back, startled by Jesse's boisterous tone. "Me. You said you have no weaknesses, yet your magic has its limits. Limited magic is a weakness."

"At least I have magic, you freak!"

Caleb giggled. "And I've never denied that. At least I can admit my weaknesses."

Jesse clenched his fists and a smile stretched across the king's face as he watched this fight unfold. Caleb scowled, rage bubbling inside him. He wished he had the strength to beat this bastard to a pulp.

Shayne urged Caleb to sit down. Caleb's face was still bright red in anger as he listened to Jesse's bullshit continue to leave his mouth. He knew that at some point, if both of them were offered a place on the army, that they would end up in a fight.

The doors burst open, and two guards entered, holding their spears at their sides. They hit the base of the stick on the ground and stood professionally. Everyone in the room diverted their gaze to the guards.

"How *dare* you interrupt this private meeting!" King Bartholomew bellowed. "What reason do you have?"

"Two more recruits, Your Highness," said the guard.

The two guards moved apart from each other, and two ladies walked through the centre of them. They stood in a warrior's pose, their elbows bent and fists in the air. Caleb was impressed that two women had the courage to sign up to the army, especially when the

THE KING'S ARMY

stakes were high. But he didn't care really. At least they would have magic to utilise—unlike him.

"Is this a joke?" the king said. "Women? We can't have *women* on the army!"

"Why not, Your Highness?" asked the guard.

"Because *Andrew*, fighting is a *man's* sport. Women can't fight."

"Excuse me?" spat one of the ladies. "Do you know who you're talking to?"

"No, I don't know *who* you are. I've never seen you around before. Probably prostitutes or some shit like that. Disgusting." The king gathered spit in his mouth and spat it out, making Caleb feel sick.

Eve's mouth dropped, offended by the king's remarks. "I'm Eve, and this is Becca—" Eve pointed to the woman stood next to her— "We're both strong women. We can fight."

King Bartholomew stomped over to them. He stuck his face in Eve's and let his revolting breath float into her nostrils. "Prove it."

Caleb couldn't believe what he was seeing. Who knew the king was sexist? He wanted his daughter (a woman) saved, yet he was disgusted at the thought a woman could potentially save the princess. Maybe the tailor was right - maybe the princess was to marry her saviour. And if her saviour was a woman, the king would obviously hate that.

"Fine," said Becca. "We'll prove how good we are at fighting."

4

THE BATTLEGROUND WAS situated at the back of the palace, and it was a long walk to it. Caleb couldn't believe how big the palace really was. He turned to Shayne but didn't say anything. Instead, he just smiled in admiration. He was in the poshest, cleanest, and shiniest place in the kingdom.

"I can't believe we're actually about to witness this," whispered Shayne. "I've never seen a woman wield a sword before."

Caleb shook his head. "That's because the king bans women from participating in the sport. Women have to train in secret."

"It's horrible. I can't believe our king is a sexist pig."

Everyone walked under a passageway and entered the battleground. The sand crunched beneath their feet; the seats were empty, yet they seemed so full as the wind blew around them, causing a racket of noise. The king stopped in front of everyone, causing them to jolt to a stop.

"Eve and Becca," announced the king. "Please make your way to the centre of the battleground."

Immediately, Eve and Becca marched to the centre of the battleground and turned to face King

THE KING'S ARMY

Bartholomew. The men took their seats and watched in anticipation as the king announced what the ladies would be doing.

"First," he said, "you'll fire an arrow. There are three targets-" the king pointed to the end of the battleground, where three target boards were set up, one of them surrounded by a ring of fire— "over there and each one has a different level of difficulty. Hit the middle circle, and you've passed the first challenge."

"Piece of piss," said Becca.

She grabbed her bow and arrow and angled it at the target surrounded by fire. Without instruction, Becca fired the arrow, and it flew through the air, heading straight for the centre of the target. It hit the target with a thud, spraying fire into the air. The king was just as surprised as everyone else. Caleb couldn't believe it—these women were professionals!

"My turn," Eve said, smirking.

Eve grabbed a bow and arrow from the bucket and aimed the arrow at the target which had electric bolts around it. If the arrow flew at the wrong angle, it would be struck by a heavy bolt, sending it back to the warrior, killing them instantly. Caleb bit his fingers anxiously. Would Eve be able to do it?

She angled the arrow and let it go. It hit the centre of the target. Caleb stood up a cheered, followed by the rest of the elves around him. Eve and Becca bowed to them and smirked at the king.

"Are we in?" Eve said.

THE KING'S ARMY

King Bartholomew scowled. "Hold your horses, missus. You've still got another challenge to complete."

Eve shrugged her shoulders. "Bring it on."

Things became tense between the three. Caleb's anxiety rose as he watched the king intimidate Eve and Becca. The king took in a deep breath and circled around the two ladies. Caleb looked away, the king's circular motion making him feel dizzy.

"You must now battle," King Bartholomew announced. "You will both duel in the battleground."

"Fight against each *other?*" Eve spat. "Are you serious?"

"You must prove yourselves worthy of being in my army."

Eve looked over at the men. "Have you asked them to duel against each other?"

"Not yet, their challenges were to begin later today. But you two rudely interrupted our meeting; therefore, you will be the first to prove yourselves."

Becca huffed. "This is ridiculous."

"Ridiculous, is it?" the king roared. "Get out then!"

"No. I want to be on this army. I want to save your daughter."

"Why?"

Becca froze for a moment. Then, she spoke. "Because she's royalty. She doesn't deserve to be locked up somewhere."

The king grumbled.

Caleb stood up and marched over to the king.

THE KING'S ARMY

"Leave them alone," said Caleb.

The king lifted his arm and swung it, his hand striking Caleb's face with a strong force. "You dare approach me without permission?"

Caleb held his face, the pain racing through him. He couldn't believe the strength of the pain the king had caused him.

"They've done nothing to you," Caleb cried. "All they want to do is save your daughter because you can't be bothered to get off your arse and do it yourself!"

The king lifted Caleb in the air, his feet rising from the ground. King Bartholomew hovered in the air for a few moments before launching Caleb into the concrete palace wall. Caleb's bones crunched as he hit the wall with an almighty blow. He fell to the ground in a heap, unable to move. Caleb grumbled, spluttering, and spitting out blood. He staggered to his feet, wobbling slightly, holding onto the wall to keep his balance.

"You're a psycho," he said, coughing. "The princess deserves better."

Caleb grabbed a spear and gripped it in his hand. He wanted to throw it. He urged himself to throw it. But he just couldn't do it.

"Go on," the king said. "Throw it."

Caleb screwed up his face and threw the spear. It didn't go much further than a few feet in front of him. Everyone in the battleground roared with laughter. Except for Eve and Becca, who only let out a light giggle. Caleb looked around at everyone, embarrassed by his performance. He *needed* to get better at this.

THE KING'S ARMY

He sat back down next to Shayne, scowling. The king was an awful man.

Eve and Becca eventually agreed to duel against each other, although they had made the rule of no harm coming to either of them. They climbed into their battle gear and the duel began. Their roars echoed around the battleground as they charged towards each other. Eve and Becca's swords met each other, scraping like nails on a chalkboard. The army grimaced at the sound, covering their ears. The ladies pulled their swords away from each other and swung them, deliberately missing each other's bodies so not to cause any injuries. Again, they brought their swords close.

Caleb flinched at the sound of the swords smashing against each other, the clang echoing throughout the battleground. It was a very underwhelming duel, but it was enough for the king to be impressed. And it took a *lot* to impress the king. Caleb thought King Bartholomew would be crazy not to allow these two ladies onto his army. After all, if he wasn't going to save his own daughter then he was going to need all the help he could get.

c⚜⁾

The sun sizzled in the sky across the battleground, shining in everyone's faces. Caleb squinted his eyes trying to block the light. King Bartholomew made his way to the centre of the battleground and made an announcement.

THE KING'S ARMY

"It is now time for you all to prove whether you're worthy for the King's Army," he said. "Firstly, one by one, you will each come up to me and tell me what weapon you'd most like to wield, what your magic is, and how you intend to use both of these in battle."

Shit. Caleb didn't have a clue what weapon he wanted, nor did he know how he would use it in battle. And he didn't have any magic either. This was it. There was no way the king would choose him for the army now.

Jesse was the first elf to go up to the king—of course he was. He was so full of himself, and Caleb hated him for it. Caleb looked at Shayne and rolled his eyes, waiting for Jesse to start spewing his usual bullshit.

"I'd most like to use the morning star," said Jesse. "I love the appearance of it, and I know it will do some serious damage. My magic is teleportation. I can use both of these in battle by teleporting from one place to the other quickly, meaning I have less chance of being attacked and I can sneak up on people and strike them with my weapon before they even have the chance to dodge and fight with me."

The king grunted. "Very good. Next." He pointed to Shayne.

"Bollocks," muttered Shayne. He stood up and walked over to the king.

"You may begin," said King Bartholomew.

THE KING'S ARMY

Shayne paused. Caleb watched as his friend stood in silence, not saying anything. He wondered if Shayne was going to be able to do this.

"Speak!"

Shayne flinched. "Erm...my magic allows me to hover. I can float in the air. I'd like to use a sword - basic, I know. I'm a basic bitch. Anyway, I'm not sure how I can use both in battle to be honest. Maybe I can float in the air to avoid any damage from other weapons?"

The king grunted again. Caleb wasn't sure what to think of this. Was the king impressed with Shayne, or had he decided that Shayne would *not* be on the army? Caleb wasn't sure, but he hoped that whatever happened with Shayne, he had the same result. At least he'd be able to stick with his best friend no matter what.

"You may sit down. Next!" the king boomed.

Nobody moved. Caleb looked around him, hoping someone would go up soon. But nobody did. The king's finger pointed towards him. *Oh no.*

Caleb stood up and trudged over to the king. "I'll be honest, I—"

"Did I say you can speak?" roared King Bartholomew.

Caleb shook his head.

"You may now speak."

Caleb rolled his eyes, disgruntled at the king's attitude. "I don't really know much about weapons, and I have no magic. I was born without it, it's a rare genetic disorder. But I'd love to use this as an opportunity to prove to you and everyone else in the kingdom

THE KING'S ARMY

that I can do things that everyone else can do, just with a few minor differences and challenges."

The elves around him giggled to themselves. Caleb knew they didn't have any faith in him. He worried that the king didn't have any faith in him either and would dismiss him from the palace there and then.

"Finished?" the king asked.

"Yes."

"Be seated."

༄

It was past sunset by the time Caleb returned home. He knew he was in trouble with his mum. Opening the front door slowly, Caleb sneaked into the house. The snap of a matchstick startled him, and the room began to glow by candlelight.

"Where have you been all day?" Meredith asked.

"Out with Shayne," said Caleb.

"That doesn't answer my question. I asked *where* you've been. Not who you've been with."

Caleb grumbled. "I've been at the palace. I've signed up for the King's Army."

"You what?!" Meredith screamed.

She jumped up from her seat, sending the candle flying across the room. It landed on a rag on the floor, instantly lighting it up. The room burst into flames, the scorching heat slapping Caleb in the face.

"Mum!" Caleb roared. "Mum, you need to get out!"

THE KING'S ARMY

"Jasmine!" Meredith cried.

Caleb rushed up the stairs and burst into his sister's bedroom, where she lay asleep. He lifted her and carried her down the stairs, rushing past the flames and out into the street. He and Meredith watched as their house rapidly burned. Caleb saw Jasmine's eyes flicker.

"What's happening?" she asked, still half asleep.

"It's okay," said Caleb. "We're safe."

5

SINCE THE FIRE, Caleb and his family had been sleeping in a small hut on the edge of the village. There was nowhere else for them to stay; their community didn't want to help them because they considered Caleb a degenerate.

"If you're accepted onto the army," Meredith said to Caleb, "then you *need* to make sure there will be a financial benefit from it because we can't stay here forever. Your sister can't sleep on that floor."

Caleb frowned. He knew the fire was his fault. If he hadn't signed up for the army, then his mother wouldn't have got angry; and if his mother hadn't got angry, then the fire wouldn't have started. This all led back to him.

"This is all my fault," said Caleb, a small tear dripping from his eye. "I'm so sorry, Mum."

Meredith held her finger against Caleb's lips. "Don't blame yourself. Just get on with whatever it is you need to do. We'll talk about everything else when you return home."

The Messenger hurried along the pathway and approached Caleb and his family. "The king is making an announcement. He has chosen his army recruits, and

THE KING'S ARMY

everyone must gather in the Garden of Kate immediately."

He raced off deeper into the village. Caleb and his family rushed to the Garden of Kate to find out whether he had been accepted onto the army and if the kingdom would finally have some faith in him.

※

The elves of the Shihan Kingdom gathered in the garden, muttering amongst themselves whilst they awaited the king. A dragon hovered above and dived down into the garden. Everyone ducked as the dragon skimmed along their heads. It landed on the other side and King Bartholomew approached his stand.

"Good morning," said the king. "I've gathered you all here so I can introduce you to my army."

The Garden of Kate was silent.

"I'll cut to the chase. If you hear your name, please come to the front."

Caleb waited in anticipation as he heard the king call his recruits up. Jesse, Tobias, Damien, Eve, Becca, Lewis...

"Shayne Beckett...Henry Hughes..."

Two more names and the army would be complete. Caleb bit his fingernails. The ninth name was called out - Milo.

I haven't made it onto the army.

"And finally..."

THE KING'S ARMY

Come on. Please say my name.
"...please could..."
Please.
"Caleb Fischer come to the front!"

Caleb's stomach dropped. He couldn't believe it. Shock was obvious on his face, but he was delighted that the king believed in him. As he walked up to the front, everyone in the garden scowled at him. It was obvious they didn't think he was worthy of being on the army.

"Please give a cheer for my army!" the king bellowed.

The crowd cheered as King Bartholomew called out the names of the army recruits, but they fell silent when Caleb's name was shouted out. But he didn't care what everyone else thought. He was going to work hard, train hard, and prove to the king that he was worthy of a blessing.

"Whoever rescues my little girl will not only have a royal house that is being built within the palace, but they will also marry her!" King Bartholomew announced.

Caleb looked at Eve and Becca. Could they marry Princess Kate? He didn't believe that the king would accept that, and he wasn't sure if the princess would even *want* to marry a woman. But there was only one way to find out. Caleb wasn't fussed about marrying her though—his motivation was the royal house. If he rescued Kate, he could give his mother and sister a

THE KING'S ARMY

new home. A home that is much better than the one they used to live in.

King Bartholomew ushered his army out of the garden. Caleb looked back. He guessed this was him off to the palace for the foreseeable future. Not even a chance to say goodbye to his mother and sister.

"You'll each be escorted to the palace via a dragon, each one assigned to you by me. We shall meet in the battleground," said the king.

A swarm of dragons hovered above, before they gently flew towards everyone and landed on the grass, squishing it beneath their scaly, clawed feet.

The elves approached their assigned dragon and hopped into its back, before being taken off into the air. Caleb straddled his dragon and held onto the harness, ensuring not to let go. He didn't want to fall from a great height - that would be fatal! The dragon took off and glided through the air, the wind hitting against Caleb's face. Caleb quite enjoyed the ride; more than he thought he would. Clouds drifted past him, their soft touch tickling his skin. Before he knew it, he arrived at the palace, the dragon landing in the battleground with a hard thump, rocking everything around. Caleb struggled off the dragon's back and strode over to the other elves.

"How was the ride?" Shayne asked.

"It was fun," said Caleb. "I quite enjoyed it to be honest."

THE KING'S ARMY

Damien wandered over to the pair and smirked, slapping Caleb's back. "What's happening, Magic-less Mongrel?"

"Excuse me?" Caleb snapped. "Who the hell do you think you're talking to?"

"You. You have no place on this army. You're useless. Do you seriously think you'll last five minutes in here?"

"I'll do what it takes to last the entire time!"

Damien chuckled. "You'll never make it. You have no magic, you're not strong enough, and you're poor. No wonder your sister is going to be forever a cripple."

Caleb grabbed Damien by the collar and pushed him to the ground. "Say one more word about my sister and you'll be *dead*."

Damien showed no remorse. Instead, he just laughed in Caleb's face as he struggled to his feet. Just as he was about to retaliate, Damien was interrupted by the boom of King Bartholomew's voice. The king came through from the archway and made his way to the centre of the battleground. Everyone formed a line and waited for the king to speak.

"You will spend tomorrow training for battle. Just one day. Anyone who isn't prepared will be putting themselves at risk; I have no time for the slow ones," said King Bartholomew.

Sweat dripped down Caleb's forehead. He knew it would take more than a day for him to learn how to

THE KING'S ARMY

fight. There was absolutely no way he would be able to do it all in one day.

"You will then board the ship," the king continued, "and you'll sail to the Ice Kingdom where you will then fight to save my daughter."

The elves looked at each other, but their eyes stopped on Caleb.

"What?" Caleb snapped.

"You better not let us down, shit-dick," growled Jesse. "We know what you are."

Caleb scowled. "Do one."

6

THE ARMY WOKE in the palace, the sun glaring off the stained-glass window. Caleb rubbed his tired eyes and looked over at Shayne who was still asleep. He wanted to leave the palace. It wasn't the nicest place to be, especially the room they were all sleeping in. Caleb looked at the other elves who were all sitting in silence, scowling at the grubby floor. Considering they were all about to risk their lives for the princess, King Bartholomew didn't have much respect for them.

"I think we should come up with a plan for battle," said Caleb.

"Shut up," replied Lewis. "You'll be the first killed anyway so there's no point in you having an opinion on any of it."

"You need to start having a bit more respect for me!"

"Or what? What're you gonna do about it?"

Caleb stood up and stomped over to where Lewis was sitting and attempted to kick him directly in the face. Lewis pushed his hand out, blasting energy towards Caleb, throwing him back against the wall.

"See what I mean?" Lewis snarled. "There is no way you're going to survive this. I don't even know why the king recruited you in the first place."

THE KING'S ARMY

Caleb struggled to his feet. "Well, he obviously has faith in me. More than you guys do."

"Of course, we don't have faith in you," Eve interjected. "You're a lovely lad but you're pretty useless to us. You can't do anything like we can."

"Who asked for your opinion?" Caleb snapped.

"The princess isn't going to want you."

"I don't care if she does or doesn't. I'm here to prove I'm just as worthy as anyone else."

"So am I!"

Everyone fell silent. Caleb knew that nobody had faith in him, and he knew he was most likely going to let everybody down. But he wasn't going to let their opinions get on top of him. He'd ignore them and do his thing. He would prove them wrong.

༄

The Weapons Room was located on the other side of the palace, at the very end of a large corridor decorated with royal portraits and bannisters made of real gold. Caleb twitched as a golden sparkle glimmered in his eye.

"This is amazing," whispered Shayne. "I can't believe we're finally here."

Caleb grumbled. "Shame we're not being treated this well considering we're all putting our lives on the line for *his* daughter."

"True. But still, one of us will marry the princess, *and* we get to give her a good sausage too."

THE KING'S ARMY

"Shayne, we might die. Don't get your hopes up about shagging the princess when we haven't even started the battle yet."

Shayne smirked. "Well, if I don't get the princess then I might make a go on the prince."

Caleb slapped his friend around the back of his head and laughed. "You are such a whore."

Shayne chuckled as they headed into the Weapons Room. They were instantly greeted by large cases around each wall, each one holding several weapons. Caleb was drawn straight away to the case full of flails. The idea of swinging a spiky ball on a chain at someone's face filled him with joy. He would make sure he got to use that. Maybe he could use it on some of his fellow army warriors since they seem to enjoy making a mockery of him. That would soon teach them.

The army formed a line and waited for their mentor to enter the room. Caleb looked around anxiously, each elf standing tall and busting their chests out like a gorilla. Then, a large built man burst into the room.

"Hello, cock-wombles!" he boomed. "I finally get to meet the idiots who signed up for this atrocity."

"What do you mean, *atrocity*?" Jesse asked.

"Do you *really* think His Highness will appreciate what you're going to do? He's just too lazy to do it himself so he hires the peasants of the kingdom."

"I am no peasant."

"You live in a tiny hut in the centre of the village, and you still have your mother living with you."

THE KING'S ARMY

Caleb watched as the mentor continued to rip into Jesse. It was the least he deserved. When the mentor had finished, he turned to the rest of the group.

"My name is Tylor and I'll be your mentor today. I'll teach you everything you need to know about weaponry and dragon taming," said the mentor. "The time is now 9am, you'll finish training at 10pm. There is a long day ahead so *no* slacking. I don't have time for that shit."

A lump formed in Caleb's throat, dread welling up inside him. He didn't like Tylor all that much — except when he was ripping into Jesse.

"So, who wants to come up first?" Tylor asked.

Before anyone else could, Shayne pushed his way through the others and approached Tylor. Jesse growled and clenched his fists. Of course, *he* wanted to be first. What a cock.

"Name?" Tylor asked.

"Shayne."

Caleb paid close attention to what Tylor was saying to Shayne, listening intensely to the descriptions of each weapon. When Tylor got to the flail, Caleb's ears perked up. Now *this* was where it would get interesting. Caleb had a strong like for the flail ever since he had arrived at the palace. He knew it could cause some serious damage and that's what he loved about it. Caleb knew he could easily kill some of the warriors from the Ice Kingdom and could potentially kill some of his fellow army warriors too, particularly Jesse. He was the biggest arsehole Caleb had ever met.

THE KING'S ARMY

"The flail is a weapon you need to use carefully," said Tylor, "because the ball is lethal. One swift strike and you're dead. So, when you're swinging it towards the enemy, make sure it is away from your head."

Shayne took hold of the flail and stared at it adoringly. Caleb could tell that this was going to be Shayne's choice of weapon. And he was glad about it because that would mean he'd be able to work closely with his best friend to fight for the princess. Shayne stood back in line and the next elf to go over to Tylor was Damien. Someone else Caleb didn't like much.

"I'd love to learn more about crossbows," said Damien. "I think they're so cool!"

Tylor didn't crack a smile. "Slow down. I haven't even started yet."

Caleb giggled as he watched Tylor drag Damien to each section of the Weapons Room, talking him through each one. Unfortunately, Caleb would be hearing the same information multiple times and then he'd be hearing it again properly when it becomes his turn to go up. But watching Damien feel intimidated by Tylor gave Caleb a sense of joy.

⁂

It soon became Caleb's turn to go up and have the weapons tour. Hearing the same information repeatedly became incredibly boring for him, but it also meant he would remember it which gave him a huge advantage.

THE KING'S ARMY

"Which weapon are you most interested in?" Tylor asked.

Caleb looked at the array of weapons, pretending to think hard. But he already knew which weapons he wanted to know more about—the flail, and the crossbow. Both weapons had some great advantages to them, and he was determined to get the chance to use both, even if for a short while.

"I'd like to learn more about the flail and the crossbow," said Caleb, "I think they're both amazing."

"Very well." Tylor picked up the flail. "Handle this very carefully." He handed it to Caleb.

Caleb took the flail from Tylor and held it delicately, making sure not to drop it or injure himself with it.

"It's heavier than I thought," Caleb said with a laugh. "Gonna have to train me hard on this."

"Stop trying to make small talk. Now watch."

Tylor held the handle with both of his hands and swung it back behind his shoulders. He swung it forwards, smashing onto the tabletop, ripping the wood from it. Caleb jumped back, startled by the loud bang it made.

"This is how much damage the flail can do," said Tylor. "Now do you see why I said to make sure to keep the ball *away* from your head?"

Caleb nodded. "Yes."

"Right, now it's your turn to do it."

"Do what?"

THE KING'S ARMY

"Wield the weapon, arsehole!" Tylor roared. "Do exactly what I just did!"

Caleb glared at Tylor for a few moments before copying what he did. Caleb stretched the flail behind his shoulders and swung it forward, launching it towards the table. But the weight became too much for him, and he ended up letting go of the weapon before he managed to bring it fully down. The flail rocketed towards Tylor, striking him in the chest and knocking him dead instantly, blood pouring from the deep wound Caleb had just caused.

"Shit!" Caleb screamed. "Oh, *shit!*"

The army crowded around Tylor, horrified yet somewhat impressed. Caleb flapped his arms around in a panic, flitting his head back and forth between everyone in the room. He sought guidance; needed someone to tell him what to do.

"What do I do?" Caleb said.

"Run," replied Milo.

And in an instant, Milo had disappeared, darting out the door. The other elves froze for a moment before also making the decision to run, leaving Caleb and Shayne alone.

"Christ, how did you do that?" Shayne said, nervously laughing.

Caleb lifted his brow. "I don't know, the flail was too heavy, and I just let go of it by accident. I didn't mean to kill him."

"Don't panic, we'll sort this out."

THE KING'S ARMY

"And how are we going to do that? He's dead and if the king finds out I killed one of his staff, then he'll kill *me!*"

Shayne patted his friend's back, comfortingly. "Leave it with me."

※

"What did you do with the body?"

Shayne pulled Caleb behind a wall. "I buried him."

"You did what?"

"I buried him. Funnily enough, that's what you do with dead bodies."

Caleb rolled his eyes. "I know that! But *how?*"

"I put his body into a potato sack and carried it out of the palace and into the gardens. There's an allotment in there so it was the perfect place."

"How did you not get caught?"

Shayne giggled. "The garden once belonged to the king's wife. No one has been there since she died, so it was easy to go in and not get caught."

Caleb's heart raced and his breathing became heavier. Taking in deep breaths, Caleb managed to calm himself down eventually. He couldn't believe what he had done and what his friend had done to solve the issue. Guilt spread within him.

"Stop panicking!" Shayne spat. "Otherwise, the king will find out. This proves that you can do this. You can be a successful warrior in the army."

THE KING'S ARMY

Caleb shook his head. "I didn't want to kill our mentor though. Now none of us will learn anything because Tylor was the only mentor."

"Shit."

"Yeah, *shit.*"

Shayne looked around the corner. Nobody was there except for a few guards wandering around the courtyard.

"Just please try not to panic any more. Don't bring attention to yourself, do what you came here to do, and forget any of this happened. Forget where I've buried Tylor."

Caleb nodded. "Okay."

They walked back from behind the wall and went back into the palace. The rest of the army greeted them and smirked at Caleb.

"How does it feel to be a killer?" Jesse said. "Didn't think you had it in you!"

"I don't," mumbled Caleb.

"Ignore him," Shayne said. "My friend is strong, and he is a capable warrior. You all need to start having more faith in him."

"He killed our mentor," Becca piped in. "Without him, we have no chance of knowing much else."

"You're a capable warrior; you proved that in the battleground the other day. You don't need a mentor, Becca. Stop being a dick."

Becca stormed towards Shayne, failing to attack him as he floated into the air.

THE KING'S ARMY

"Get your arse down here, now!" Becca screamed. "Nobody talks to me like that without consequences."

"Get over it."

Shayne floated down, tripping Becca as she lunged towards him. Becca flew across the floor and crashed into the table at the side of the wall. She groaned in pain. Shayne strutted off, heading towards the bedroom. Caleb smirked, impressed by Shayne's unexpected strength.

Becca struggled to her feet, wiping her nose with the back of her hand, blood smearing across it. She spat on the ground.

"You'll regret that," she said. "I'll kill you."

"You can't kill me, we're on the same side. We need to kill those in the Ice Kingdom," Shayne said, sarcastically.

"I can kill who I want, no one can stop me."

"His Highness won't be happy."

"I don't give a *shit* what he thinks!"

Everyone turned around at the sound of someone clearing their throat.

The king.

He stood at the top of the staircase, before slowly making his way down, one step at a time. The army stood to attention and waited for King Bartholomew to make his way to the bottom of the staircase.

"What's all the commotion down here?" he boomed.

"Becca's being a gobby bitch," said Shayne.

THE KING'S ARMY

"Will you shut the hell up?!" Becca screamed. "I'm sick of you and your dickhead mate."

"Leave me out of this," Caleb piped in.

"Will you *all* shut up and stop arguing?!" King Bartholomew barked. "I'm beginning to regret recruiting some of you."

Everyone fell silent.

The king grunted. "Now where is Tylor?"

Caleb's stomach dropped. He felt sick. A lump formed in his throat, but he gulped it down. The king couldn't find out what happened. Caleb would probably be killed if the king knew what he had done.

Shayne glanced over at Caleb.

"Don't know," said Shayne, before anyone else could tell the truth. "He left us and didn't come back."

"Useless prick," the king grumbled. "I knew I should have dismissed him a long time ago. So, are you all ready for the big day tomorrow?"

"No!" Milo yelled. "We've had no training. It's all his fault."

Milo went to point at Caleb, but Shayne pulled his arm down, causing Milo to scream out in pain. The king looked at the army, confusion settling in.

"Who's fault?" King Bartholomew asked.

"Tylor's," Caleb said abruptly. "He left us, so we have no training."

The king threw his hands in the air, angrily. "Guess I'll have to train you all myself! Follow me!"

THE KING'S ARMY

The army followed King Bartholomew back to the Weapon's Room and gathered around the weapon's cabinet. The king browsed the selection of weapons and pulled one out, presenting it to the army.

"This sword," said the king, "is the most powerful sword in the kingdom."

The army gawped at it. Caleb wasn't sure how it was exactly the most powerful, but he kind of wanted to use it. Then, the king placed it back in the cabinet and secured it shut.

"Do not touch that sword," King Bartholomew barked.

Caleb stumbled backwards, startled by the king's tone. The king handed each elf a weapon and showed them, one by one, how to use it. Caleb was anxious about King Bartholomew getting to him. He didn't want to be taught by the king—he was scared about revealing he was responsible for Tylor's death.

7

THE RESIDENTS OF the Shihan Kingdom gathered at the harbour. A large ship was docked by the edge, the sails flapping furiously in the wind. As the army emerged from the palace down to the harbour, the elves roared in celebration—all except for Meredith and Jasmine. Caleb could see them looking at him, dismay written across their faces. He began to have regrets about joining the King's Army, but he needed that gold. His family needed a home. The army stopped in their tracks and turned towards the crowd.

"Elves of the Shihan Kingdom!" King Bartholomew bellowed. "Please give a loud cheer for your army!"

Everyone cheered, waving their arms in the air, and jumping up and down. The king called out each of the warrior's names, but the crowd fell silent when he called out Caleb's name. Caleb frowned. Why didn't anyone believe in him? He believed the rest of the army were beginning to have faith in him now that he had killed Tylor. Although the murder was an accident, he still did it. And that was all that mattered to him. He proved he could kill; of course, he was going to take credit for it, accident or not.

THE KING'S ARMY

The King's Army marched down to the ship and boarded it, stepping onto the top deck, and looking over the edge. They stood to attention before saluting the king. A strong gust of wind shook the boat, knocking Caleb backwards slightly. He gathered his balance and continued his salute. King Bartholomew ended the salute, followed by the army. Caleb stepped back from the side of the ship. He couldn't bear the look on his mother and sister's faces. His guilt ripped through him. Caleb sat down on the bench and buried his head in his hands. He couldn't do this.

"Wait," said Caleb.

He dashed down the steps to the bottom deck, but it was too late. The guards were securing the door closed. *Shit*. He was trapped. Now, he had no choice.

"What's up with you?" Shayne called, approaching Caleb at the bottom of the steps.

Caleb frowned, shaking his head. "I don't want to do this anymore. My mum and sister need me."

"Mate, they need you to do this and save the princess. You all need a new home. This is the only way you'll be able to do it."

"But this shouldn't be the way!" Tears fell down Caleb's face. "It's not fair that us poor people get overlooked, while all the rich bastards get everything handed to them on a plate!"

Shayne wrapped his arms around Caleb. "Come on, mate. It won't be that bad. All you've got to do is keep your head down and save the princess. Then,

THE KING'S ARMY

you're in. You'll get a wife, some kids, and a posh new home for you and your family."

"I don't want to do it."

Caleb pulled away from Shayne's grip and rushed up the steps and peered over the edge. They were in the centre of the ocean. He hadn't even realised they'd left. His village seemed miles away now; everyone grew smaller and smaller as the ship floated further away. He cursed loudly, startling everyone with his screams.

"Oh, stop being such a wet rag," Jesse mocked. "You knew what you were getting yourself into."

"Piss off!" Caleb bellowed.

The village was pulling further away. Caleb could no longer see his mother and sister. He wouldn't see them for days, maybe even weeks. Or if he's *really* unlucky, never again. The temptation to jump off the ship and swim back to the village was growing, but he dismissed his thoughts; mostly because he couldn't swim that well.

He entered the army to prove to everyone that he could fight; that he was worthy of the king's blessing. There was no way he could drop out.

"You need to calm down," said Shayne, approaching Caleb. "You can't let all the emotions of this get to you."

Caleb buried his head between his knees. "I can't do it. There's no way I'll survive."

"But you *might*. Put your mind to it and you'll be fine. You can't give up."

THE KING'S ARMY

"And what if I do give up?"

"Then you'll be proving everyone else right. You'll be showing that you can't do it."

Caleb lifted his head and looked at Shayne. He knew his friend was right. There was no way he could let everyone say, "I told you so," and mock him for the rest of his life. He'll be known as the army dropout. Jesse and his mob would laugh at him every time they walked past him.

"You're right," said Caleb. "I need to do this."

Shayne tapped his hand on Caleb's back. "Good lad. Now, we have a day long trip to the Ice Kingdom, so we may as well find a way to entertain ourselves."

"By doing what?"

Shayne glared at Caleb, looking him up and down, licking his lips.

"No!" Caleb snapped, edging away from Shayne. "No way."

"What?" Shayne asked. "It's just a bit of fun, doesn't have to mean anything"

"There is *no way* we're doing that. That's not who I am. I accept you for who you are, but it's not me. Plus, we're best friends. It will be weird."

Shayne giggled. "Mate, I'm messing with you. I'm not serious. But we should find something to do to keep ourselves occupied. There's no way we can sit here for a day doing nothing."

Caleb grumbled. "No."

He walked away from Shayne and went down to the lower deck. It didn't smell particularly nice, but he

THE KING'S ARMY

needed to be alone, away from everyone else. Visions of his mother's desperate face flashed through his mind. His mind flashed back to the fire. The house destroyed, burnt to a crisp. Something in him clicked; he didn't know what, but it urged him to go back to the top deck and be with everyone else. He approached the army and sat with them. They were discussing their battle plan, how they would sneak through the kingdom without being killed.

"Does anyone here have invisibility powers?" Caleb asked.

"I do," said Damien.

"What are the limits?"

"I can't make people invisible, but I can make myself and small objects invisible."

"So that's kind of okay. Not convenient that we can't disguise the ship, but if you disguise our weapons, we could potentially attack the Ice Kingdom's army."

"That won't work," said Lewis. "They'll still see us. If we go near them, we're basically offering our lives to them."

Jesse laughed in Caleb's face. "Stupid dick with stupid ideas!"

Rage fuelled within Caleb, but he calmed himself down. There was no way he could beat Jesse, so instead, he walked over to the edge of the ship, looking over. Mountains appeared in the distance, disguised by fog. The Shihan Kingdom was miles away, the village even further. Caleb frowned. He missed his family. His mother's words rang in his ears.

THE KING'S ARMY

You caused this. This is your fault.

He knew the fire was his fault. Joining the army was his way of rectifying his terrible, *terrible* mistake — a mistake that could have been fatal.

Although it was foggy, Caleb could still see the inhabitants going about their daily lives. A small village by the ocean was rammed with elves, a market running up the dusty pathway. Caleb smiled. It reminded him of the Shihan Kingdom when he was a child before the Khrishan War hit. After that, the kingdom was never the same.

"Caleb!" Damien roared. "Get your arse over here, we're going to play a game."

"I'm alright," said Caleb. "I don't want to play."

"Suit yourself."

Whilst everyone else got involved in the game, Caleb watched the world go by. There wasn't much to see except mountains and water, the odd tree here and there, and the sky constantly changing from blue to grey just before a storm started.

"We should get to the lower deck," said Lewis. "Close the hatch, we can't allow any water to get in."

The King's Army made their way to the lower deck. Whilst down there, they decided to explore the sleeping area. There were no beds. Just a blanket and pillow each. King Bartholomew hadn't gone all out to treat his army well. Caleb picked up a blanket and grunted, disgusted by its texture. He wasn't going to sleep well on this ship. The rest of the army assigned themselves a sleeping spot and wrapped their blankets around them, the cold air brushing through the deck. Furiously, the rain hammered against the ship, thunder roaring loudly, and the water beginning to swirl. The ship rose with the waves and came crashing back down, knocking the elves all over the place.

"Shit," said Jesse. "This storm isn't going to go away any time soon."

"I hope it goes soon," replied Damien. "Can't be dealing with this."

Caleb grumbled. "This is nothing compared to what we're about to face."

Jesse clenched his fists. "You've done nothing but complain since we left the village. If that's all you're going to do, why are you here?"

"To prove myself."

"The only way you'll prove yourself is if you stop being such a little bitch. We all need to work together."

Caleb laughed. "All you've done since I signed up is ridicule me! And now you're talking about working together?"

"Yeah, well, I had my reasons. But now, I realise that without teamwork, we'll fail. If I'm honest, I just want to shag the princess," said Jesse, bluntly.

"That's a disgusting reason to be here," Shayne said. "Yeah, she's a gorgeous lady. But that is no way to speak of royalty."

"Pipe down."

Shayne opened his mouth to speak but Caleb shot him a look that told him to stay quiet. There was

THE KING'S ARMY

no point everyone arguing again. Caleb rummaged around in his bag and pulled out a game of cards.

"Why don't we all play this?" Caleb suggested. "It's a good way to kill the time."

"I suppose," said Milo. "What is it?"

"Cards. I've always been a huge fan of this game; I always play it with my sister. It keeps her sane."

He distributed the cards to each member of the army as they sat in a circle, ready to play the game. Caleb started the game, placing a card in the centre of their circle—a Queen card.

"Hold on," said Shayne. "What are the rules of this game?"

Caleb began explaining the rules and the army soon got themselves involved in the game, actually enjoying each other's company and getting on great. It wasn't until Lewis won the game that everyone started arguing.

"Cheater," muttered Milo.

"How did I cheat?" Lewis snapped.

Milo didn't answer. He was just a sore loser. Caleb gathered up the cards and put them back in the box.

Silence.

The storm had since calmed down outside, and the army made their way back to the top deck. Its slippery surface caused Caleb to stumble and fall flat on his arse. He clambered to his feet and looked into the distance. It was nothing but clouds. Cold, stormy air brushed over his face, blowing the curls in his hair.

THE KING'S ARMY

"Look!" Caleb yelled, pointing to the far distance.

Everyone looked to where Caleb was pointing. A mountain covered in snow could be seen in the distance. Icy ground was just about visible. They were close. The Ice Kingdom was just a few miles away.

"I thought it would take a day to get there," said Shayne.

"The storm obviously pushed us further and faster," Caleb replied.

"Bollocks, this means we need to prepare for battle right now!" roared Jesse. "Everyone, grab your weapons and practice!"

The army raced down the steps, some slipping on the wetness, and grabbed their weapons from the side of the ship. Caleb picked up his flail, staring proudly at the spiked ball. He couldn't wait to start.

8

THE SHIP CAME to a slow halt and docked on the edge of the Ice Kingdom. The army climbed to the top deck and took in their surroundings, amazed by what they saw. For a kingdom full of crappy people and war, it was a delightful sight. Trees were dotted around, decorated with thick layers of snow. Mountains stood tall in the background, towering over everyone, making them feel small. Caleb ducked as an arrow shot towards him, skidding across his curly hair, and slamming into the mast of the ship.

"Shit!" shrieked Caleb. "We're already under attack."

More arrows were fired towards the ship, flying through the cold air and sticking into the tree bark. The army crawled along the deck and down the stairs. The door opened and they marched out, keeping low and trying to disguise themselves as much as possible. But it felt impossible. Caleb didn't have the best weapon to use from a distance. Milo, however, had a crossbow. Milo aimed his weapon towards the wintery bushes and fired it, the army hearing a loud shriek of agony as the arrow disappeared into the leaves.

"Good shot," said Caleb.

THE KING'S ARMY

Arrows stopped being fired, much to the army's relief. They walked around the side of the ship, still crouching. Jesse decided to take control, much to Caleb's dismay. Although he and Jesse were beginning to get along, he couldn't stand the thought of Jesse telling him what to do and where to be.

"We'll split up," Jesse whispered. "Half of us go that way—" Jesse pointed towards his left— "and half of us will go that way—" Jesse pointed to his right.

Everyone agreed and went in opposite directions. Caleb went to the left with Shayne, Milo, Damien, and Jesse. He leapt behind a bush, an arrow just avoiding the tip of his hair. Instead, the arrow shot straight into Damien's arm.

"Don't pull it out," said Caleb. "Leave it in your arm. We'll head back to the ship and get some bandages."

Damien wobbled, feeling faint.

"Don't pass out, either."

It was too late. Damien hit the ground like a plank of wood, blood pouring from his arm.

"Shit," said Milo. "What do we do?"

"We need to get him back to the ship. Grab his arms. I'll grab his legs."

Milo took hold of Damien's arms and Caleb took hold of Damien's legs and they carried him to the ship, carefully avoiding any weaponry that came to harm them. As they reached the ship, another arrow flew towards them, smashing through the sails, ripping huge holes in them.

THE KING'S ARMY

"Come on," whispered Caleb.

The two men carried Damien onto the ship and laid him flat on the floor. Caleb rushed around trying to find a basket full of first aid equipment. He found two rolls of bandages and unrolled one of them before wrapping it tightly around Damien's arm, keeping the wound from bleeding out even more.

"Hopefully he will wake up soon," said Milo, "otherwise I have no idea what we're going to do."

Caleb scurried around, worrying about how he was going to care for his new friend. He tried to find something— anything—to wake Damien up and to make sure he was going to be okay.

"I wish we had a healer," Caleb muttered, sadly.

"I'm a healer," a soft voice said.

Caleb and Milo turned around, greeted by a young woman stood at the ship's doorway. Her bouncy, curled hair wobbled in the light breeze, landing delicately against her pale skin. Caleb looked her up and down, instantly taken in by her beauty. Her long-sleeved dress seemed snug enough to keep her warm, but to also look presentable.

"Who are you?" Caleb asked, snapping out of his instant attraction to her.

The young woman stepped closer and crouched down, examining Damien's injuries. "My name is Matilda. I'm one of three healers in the Ice Kingdom. Your turn."

"What?"

"Who are you, and why are you here?"

9

MATILDA DIDN'T REMOVE the bandages Caleb had applied to Damien's wounds, but she did adjust them and made them stronger and more secure. Caleb hadn't done a terrible job, but he didn't do a life-saving job either.

"We aren't intruding," said Caleb. "Well, we are. But not for bad reasons."

"So why are you here then?" Matilda asked.

"Our king's daughter has been kidnapped by the Winter Queen. We're here to rescue her."

Matilda smirked. "You'll never find her."

"Why's that?" asked Milo. "Do you know something?"

"Me? No, I don't know anything. I'm just a healer. What I meant was, the Winter Queen hides. Once she takes something that doesn't belong to her, she'll hide with it. She won't be somewhere obvious." Matilda cleared her throat.

Caleb scowled. "That *bitch*."

"Correct. But for some reason, the elves here love her. Don't ask me why, I can't stand the woman," said Matilda. "She's an evil bitch that will do anything to get her own way. I don't know why she took your king's daughter, but there must have been a reason."

THE KING'S ARMY

"A reason?"

Matilda sighed defensively. "Again, I don't know. She does everything for a reason. A few months ago, she beheaded one of her guards in front of the entire kingdom because he betrayed her. She was married to him, but he was also shagging her sister. As soon as she found out—" Matilda used her hand to mimic a head being sliced off.

"Damn. She's that bad?" Milo asked.

"She's evil." Matilda paused, thinking for a moment. "Actually, no, she's a psycho."

Matilda stopped talking and turned to Damien. He was still passed out. She rummaged around in her small brown bag and pulled out a tiny bottle containing a blue liquid. Unscrewing the lid, Matilda took in a deep breath. Caleb watched as pale blue smoke floated out of the bottle and wafted around him. Considering it looked weird, its scent was rather nice.

"What's that?" Caleb asked.

Matilda looked at the bottle. "This is the Freeze Heal. Basically, I apply a small dose to a wound, and it will freeze it. This will stem any bleeding and further injuries and will heal within a matter of minutes. Although, it can take up to a couple of hours to work fully."

She poured a small amount of the potion onto a cotton ball and dabbed it over Damien's wound. Instantly, it began to work. Damien's wound looked cold, and it sent a shiver through Caleb. He shook, the feeling of cold giving him goosebumps all over his body. The

THE KING'S ARMY

veins in Damien's arm lit up bright blue before going back to their usual colour. And before long, Damien began to rouse from his sleep. He didn't say anything, he just flitted his eyes from left to right.

"Hey," said Matilda. "You're okay."

Damien cleared his throat. "What happened?"

"You were shot in the arm with an arrow," said Caleb. "But this lovely young lady saved you."

Damien looked over at Matilda and smiled. "Thank you."

Matilda smiled but didn't say a word. Instead, she got up and left.

"Bye then," Milo called after her.

Milo turned to Caleb, a look of confusion on his face. "Did you not find that a bit weird?"

"What do you mean?" Caleb asked.

"She's from the Ice Kingdom. We know what they're like here. For all we know, she could have been lying about everything. What was even in that potion?"

Caleb shrugged his shoulders. "I guess you're right. But Damien seems fine. Matilda seemed genuine and I don't think she would lie to us."

Milo grumbled, unsure. Caleb rolled his eyes and crouched down next to Damien. He checked out Damien's arm, inspecting every inch of it to ensure that nothing completely bad had happened.

"Looks fine to me," said Caleb. "Right, we have a princess to save."

Caleb and Milo helped Damien to his feet and guided him off the ship. They crawled across the ground, their hands digging deep into the snow. Caleb shivered and his teeth clicked together. His hands turned bright red, and he stopped, pulling his hands from the snow, and rubbing them together.

"Shit, it's freezing," he complained.

The three elves all stood and stampeded behind a bush, burying themselves in the leaves and trying to make as little noise as possible.

"Where are we heading to?" Damien asked.

"We'll need to head Northeast," said Caleb. "That's where the palace is located."

"Matilda said there's no way Princess Kate will be in the palace," said Milo.

"And what does she know? She's just a healer. You were saying just now she might not be trustworthy."

A soft voice squeaked from behind them. "Just a healer, am I?"

Caleb, Milo, and Damien turned around. Matilda was standing there, arms crossed, eyes watering.

Caleb stepped towards her. "Matilda, I-"

"Leave it." Matilda put her hand out, signalling for Caleb to stop. "I know you meant every word. Of course, I'm just a dumb blonde who doesn't know anything."

"Well, *do* you know anything?" Milo asked.

"Milo!" Caleb snapped.

"About the abduction, I mean. Do you know anything?"

"Not exactly."

THE KING'S ARMY

"And what do you mean by that?" asked Caleb.

Matilda sighed. "I often work in the palace to heal injuries sustained in battle. A few days ago, I overheard the queen discussing the abduction. She said something about the palace, and something about the Deep South."

"What's the Deep South?" Damien enquired. "It sounds scary, yet interesting."

"I'm not sure what it is exactly. All I know is that it is located further down south."

None of this made sense. The *Deep South* didn't make sense. Where was it? What was it? Was the princess there?

Caleb looked at his army friends, then looked back at Matilda. "How do we know we can trust what you're saying? You know it exists, but don't know anything about it. Seems very suspicious."

"Trust me," said Matilda, "it exists. But I must tell you this – some people don't make it out alive. It's just a matter of when you get there, and what isn't sleeping at the time."

Caleb felt like his heart dropped out his arse. "You mean, there's *beasts* or something that could kill us?"

Matilda narrowed her eyes. "That's exactly what I'm saying. And if the princess is there, she could be running out of time. If the wild dragons wake up, she doesn't have a chance."

THE KING'S ARMY

The army were in shock. Could they trust this woman? Caleb was adamant that she was right, and she was being honest. He found it odd, but he believed her.

"We should tell the others," Caleb told his friends.

⚜

"Deep South?"

"Yes, that's what Matilda said," Caleb said.

Jesse shook his head. "Never heard of it. Are you sure it *actually* exists?"

"I'm pretty sure it does."

The army were hiding in a small hut located on the edge of the kingdom, sheltered away from any enemies. It didn't smell very nice, and it was very dark, except for the faint sunlight shining through two foggy windows, one on each side of the hut. But it meant they were safe for now.

"Does anyone have a map?" Shayne asked. "That would help us find it."

Everyone shook their heads.

"Useless."

Caleb rubbed his temples, thinking hard about what their next steps should be. He had an idea. It could work. But it would be risky. And it would mean dividing the army.

"Half of us could stay here and search through the kingdom," Caleb suggested, "while the other half of us get back on the ship and search for the Deep South."

THE KING'S ARMY

"How can we possibly find the Deep South when we have no idea where it is?" Becca asked.

"That's why we have to search for it. Look in all the nooks and crannies. We'll look *everywhere*."

Jesse grunted. "It will never work."

"It will if we all work together. What do you say?"

Everyone fell silent.

Eve grabbed onto Becca, abruptly. "As long as I get to stick with Becca, I don't care whether I'm staying here or going on the search for the Deep South."

Caleb smiled. "So, you're in?"

"We have a princess to save. There's nothing to think about."

"Anyone else?" Caleb said.

Eventually, everyone else agreed. Caleb was excited. This was going to be his chance to show he could be a good leader and a competent warrior.

"So, how are we going to decide who does what?" Becca asked.

Caleb shrugged his shoulders. "Voluntary, I guess."

Everyone sighed. Jesse stood up and wandered over to a window, a slight crack shot down the centre. Caleb watched as an arrow came flying through the glass, shattering it into a hundred pieces, and lodging into Jesse's left eye. Blood spurted across the walls and stained what was left of the window. Jesse let out an agonising scream and collapsed to the floor. The army

THE KING'S ARMY

rushed over to him. Caleb held Jesse's head, keeping it still and flat on the ground.

"Help me!" Jesse cried. "Someone, please help me! Oh, the pain!"

Jesse lifted his arm to pull the arrow out of his eye socket, but Shayne held it down.

"If you do that," said Shayne, "then you're going to die."

Caleb closed his eyes and envisioned Matilda. He needed her right now. She would be able to fix this. He knew him imagining her wouldn't make her appear, but he held onto the hope that she would somehow get the message that she was needed.

"We need Matilda," said Caleb. He turned to Milo. "Go stand outside. Keep hidden. Matilda might show up."

Milo reluctantly went outside, carrying his crossbow ready to attack anyone at any given moment. Meanwhile, the rest of the army remained where they were, keeping safe and trying their best to keep Jesse alive. But they were running out of time. Jesse kept drifting in and out of consciousness. He was their strongest recruit, and their best hope of surviving this voyage. Without his strength and battle skills, the army was doomed to fail. Caleb prayed that Matilda would show up and heal Jesse's injury soon.

A painful scream echoed.

Everyone's gaze darted towards the door.

Milo.

THE KING'S ARMY

Damien crouched down and walked awkwardly over to the other window. The fogginess made it difficult to look out of, but he could just about make out the shapes of about thirty guards, spread out, marching around the hut.

"Shit," he said. "We're surrounded."

Caleb bit his tongue. He wanted to cry. He wanted to scream. The only way they were going to get out of this hut was in a body bag.

"What do we do?" Eve asked.

"We have to use the weapons we've got to fight against the guards," said Caleb. "I know not all of them are suitable in these circumstances, but we have to make do with what we've got."

The door opened, startling everyone. They all stood as still as possible.

This is the end.

A young lady stood in the doorway and slammed the door shut. "You summoned me?"

"Oh, thank God," Caleb puffed, sighing with relief. "It's you."

"Who's this?" Lewis asked.

"This is Matilda. She's a healer."

Matilda didn't bother with the small talk. She had a job to do. Caleb watched her approach Jesse. At first, Matilda didn't even touch the arrow. It was too dangerous. She rummaged around in her bag and pulled out a bandage soaked in some foul-smelling concoction. Jesse winced as Matilda dabbed the bandage

THE KING'S ARMY

around his eye, soaking up the blood and gently easing the flow.

"You might feel a little pinch," said Matilda.

Jesse didn't even have time to respond as Matilda pulled the arrow from his eye. His screams of pain echoed through the hut. Caleb jumped back. Although he couldn't physically feel the pain, he could feel it spiritually. He winched, clenching his teeth.

Ouch.

Matilda quickly placed her hand over his injured eye. She closed her eyes and muttered some words. Caleb couldn't make out what she was saying, but he figured it was some sort of spell to heal Jesse's pain and injury.

"Can you hurry this up?" snapped Jesse.

"Can you let me do my job?" Matilda replied. "This takes time and concentration."

She searched through her bag and pulled out a small bottle of red liquid. It looked foul, with small orange bubbles floating upwards. It reminded Caleb of his mother's homemade chilli dip she sometimes made when he was younger.

"What's that?" Caleb asked.

"Heat Heal," said Matilda. "Remember the Freeze Heal I used on your friend? Well, it's like that except it uses heat to heal rather than cold."

Matilda poured just a small dose of it onto a dry bandage and placed it over Jesse's eye. The smoke from the heat rose.

THE KING'S ARMY

"I think it's working," Jesse said, "but it does really burn."

"The burning sensation won't last long," explained Matilda, "but you will have a nasty red mark for a few hours."

"Well, at least I'm not dead, I suppose."

Caleb looked towards the door. He thought he should check on Milo. Right now, Milo could be dead. He looked out the window; the hut was still surrounded. Guards, dragons, and wolves all stood still. Guards had their weapons posed, the wolves were ready to pounce, and the dragons were waving their wings, ready to dart towards any enemy.

"We're not going to make it out," Caleb whispered to Shayne, "we're completely surrounded."

Shayne paced towards the door and opened it. Caleb could see through, and there he was.

Milo.

Dead.

The snow had turned a horrible shade of red. Blood. The red liquid leaked from Milo's head, holes—presumably caused by a flail—decorating his temples.

A sudden blast rocked the hut, knocking the elves down like bowling pins. Everyone screamed as they hit one wall or another. Caleb watched Shayne fly against a beam before hitting the ground. He could see Shayne's chest rising and falling—a good sign. The sound of footsteps crunching in the snow could be heard, and Caleb looked at the open door. Shadows lingered on the snow.

THE KING'S ARMY

Shit.

Shayne rolled over and picked up a crossbow. He aimed it straight ahead, shooting a guard straight in the throat.

"Holy shit!" Caleb roared. "Good shot!"

Shayne fired the crossbow again, an arrow flying straight towards a guard with a beard bushier than a jungle. It didn't shoot him though. Instead, it got stuck in his beard. Although the situation was serious, Caleb couldn't help but giggle. That was until a flock of dragons began flying towards the hut. Caleb felt a strong heat against him. Then, the hut burst into flames.

"Run!" Damien roared.

Everyone ran from the hut, weapons in their possession. Caleb looked back at Matilda who was still treating Jesse.

Shit.

He raced back and grabbed Matilda. He didn't care that he couldn't use his weapon now. All that mattered to him was keeping the healer safe. Looking back over his shoulder, he spotted Jesse standing with a struggle. Luckily for Jesse, the guards, wolves, and dragons were chasing the rest of the group. Jesse was alone. He was safe - for now. And he had his teleportation powers if he needed to use them.

Caleb ran, keeping a tight grip on Matilda's hand. She was screaming at him, telling him to let go. But Caleb didn't listen—he wanted to protect her. He hurried his pace, as more weapons fired towards him.

THE KING'S ARMY

"He's kidnapping her!" a loud, deep voice growled. "Get him!"

Caleb gasped. That's not what he was doing, he was keeping her safe. Dragons flew above him, throwing fire at him from their mouths. A blast of fire knocked him backwards, and he almost let go of Matilda. But he managed to keep a grip on her. A branch sticking out of the snow tripped Caleb, and he darted towards the ground, letting go of Matilda. She grabbed his arm and pulled him back up.

There was no time to thank her, though. Caleb tightened his grip on Matilda's wrist and started running again, a slight limp in his step.

The ship was in sight. Caleb hurried his pace. As he reached the ship, he leaped from the land straight through the entrance and dropped Matilda. She hit the ground with a thump and rolled a short distance, smashing into the barrels and rails along the side of the ship's interior. Caleb slid across the deck, slicing his hands and knees on the wood.

"I'm capable of looking after myself," Matilda snapped. "They know me here; they wouldn't have touched me."

Caleb struggled to catch his breath. "I...I just...just wanted to...help."

"I don't need your help. I don't need *anyone's* help! I'm capable of looking after myself and fighting my own battles."

"I know," said Caleb, "I'm sorry. I just panicked; I didn't want you to get hurt."

THE KING'S ARMY

Caleb and Matilda stared intently at each other. Matilda let a smile creep onto her face. Caleb knew she knew that he didn't mean any harm.

"You're a good man," said Matilda. "I know you meant well."

Caleb smiled nervously. His heart pounded, and his lips suddenly felt dry. He felt something for her—he could feel the chemistry between them. It was subtle chemistry, but he knew it was there.

Suddenly, the remainder of the army shot through the ship's entrance and slammed the door shut.

For God's sake.

"Did anyone get hurt?" Matilda asked loudly. "If so, I'm going to have to leave and heal them."

Damien looked over. "Only a few of the guards are injured. None are dead. Most of the wolves are dead, and the dragons got away."

"What do we do about the dragons?" Caleb asked. "They're nothing like our ones."

"You can't do anything," Matilda said. "The dragons here are unbeatable. Some of them are still here from The Corodian War thirty years ago."

"How do you know that?"

Matilda shied away. "My father fought in the war. He survived but was deeply wounded by it emotionally. And physically—he lost an arm and a leg. He told me he tried to fight the dragons, but they wouldn't die."

"Why did he try to fight the dragons in his own kingdom?" Shayne asked.

THE KING'S ARMY

"He didn't. The Ice Kingdom never had dragons before The Corodian War. These dragons used to live in Askia before it got destroyed in the war."

"What happened to the life there?" Caleb wondered.

"Dead. Everyone died—except the dragons."

The silence on the ship was deafening. Caleb couldn't believe what he was hearing. Immortal dragons? He'd never heard of such a thing before.

"Where's your father now?" asked Lewis. "If you don't mind me asking."

A tear tricked down Matilda's face, her eyes bright red. "He died three months ago."

"Oh God." Caleb offered a hand of comfort, rubbing Matilda's arm gently. "I'm really sorry to hear that. How did it happen?"

Matilda's face turned from an expression of sadness to a picture of hatred. "That bitch, Queen Saphielle. She killed my father."

Caleb looked over at the four other elves and gave them the 'we need to find the princess and kill the Winter Queen' look.

"Did he do something to make her do it?" Caleb asked.

Matilda took a deep breath. "Like I said earlier, she always has a reason for doing things. I don't want to talk about it."

Eve and Becca gathered around Matilda, offering some moral support, women to woman.

THE KING'S ARMY
That Winter Bitch is going to pay. She can't get away with this.

�֎

The ship glided peacefully across the water. Caleb basked in the sunlight, watching the white, fluffy clouds float through the sky. The chill of the air brushed against Caleb's body, but he was so used to it now that it didn't faze him that much. No one really knew what to do whilst they were travelling South. Some kept look out, while others chilled out.

"Where do you think the Deep South is?" Shayne asked.

"No idea. I guess we just need to keep heading south and see where we end up," said Caleb. "There might be some kind of black hole or something that takes us there."

Shayne giggled. "A black hole? You ballbag!"

"What? It's just a thought." Caleb rolled his eyes and walked away from Shayne, leaning on the edge of the ship on the opposite side. A light wind brushed across his face, turning his cheeks a light shade of pink.

A hand landed on his shoulder, startling him.

Caleb turned around and sighed, holding his hand to his chest. "Christ, you made me jump!"

Becca giggled. "Sorry. What's the matter?"

"Nothing." Caleb shied away.

"There is something wrong, I can tell."

"Read minds now, do you?"

THE KING'S ARMY

Becca smiled. "No. But I know when someone isn't quite telling the truth."

Caleb sighed, reluctant to tell her the truth. But he wanted to open up to someone. Everything was getting on top of him, and he wanted to let it all out. Maybe Becca was the best person to talk to. All the blokes were dicks—except for Shayne—but the ladies were nicer to talk to.

"I miss my mum and my sister," said Caleb. "I'm doing this for them."

"Didn't they initially *ban* you from signing up?" Becca questioned. "How could you possibly be doing this for them?"

"The fire, it was my fault. If I hadn't signed up, me and Mum wouldn't have got into that argument; and if we hadn't got into that argument, then Mum wouldn't have accidentally knocked the candle over."

"Damn. So, how does doing this help them?"

"Whoever saves the princess not only gets to marry her, but they also get a life of luxury in one of the palace apartments."

"Really?" Becca's eyes lit up.

Caleb nodded. He looked away from Becca and let a tear slip out of his left eye. This was the first time he was properly allowing himself to be emotionally vulnerable around anyone.

"See ya." Becca left Caleb's side.

Caleb flinched and turned around, but Becca had already disappeared. He spotted her going down the

THE KING'S ARMY

steps to the lower deck, her weapons secured tightly to her back. He followed.

"Becca!" Caleb called. "Why the sudden change of tone?"

"What do you mean?" Becca asked. "All I did was leave you to it."

"No, as soon as I said about living a life of luxury in the palace, you changed. You couldn't have been more disinterested in my problems."

Becca scowled. "We're all here for the same reason."

"No, we're not. You're only here to get one over on everyone."

"No, I'm not!" Becca shrieked, offended by Caleb's accusations.

Caleb grabbed his sword. "Oh really? I've noticed the way you've been acting. Every time someone mentions what you could gain from this, your attitude changes. If the princess is mentioned, you go quiet and couldn't care less."

Becca looked at the sword. Caleb's hand gripped it tighter, turning his knuckles white.

"What are you going to do with that sword?" Becca asked.

"Unless you want to die, I suggest you start talking."

Becca giggled. "I'm *really* not intimidated by you. You're not going to kill someone on the same army as you, anyway. King Bartholomew would kill *you!*"

THE KING'S ARMY

"Oh, give it up Becca, you two-faced bitch! You're not on the same army as us, you're always against us. Got to give it to you though, your acting skills are great." Caleb rose his sword to Becca's neck. "Now, give me *one* good reason why I shouldn't kill you."

Becca raised her arms and pulled them back in close to her chest. The hatch above Caleb's head slammed shut and locked. He shuddered at the noise.

"Just me and you," said Becca. "I have magic, you don't. Guess who's going to win?"

Just as Becca was about to launch herself at Caleb, the ship shook violently, sending Caleb and Becca flying into every part of the lower deck as they slipped and slid around before being thrown against the hard wood. Eventually, it calmed down.

"What the hell was that?" Caleb said.

"Who cares?" Becca grumbled. "It's not like you'll be around much longer to worry about it."

Caleb scrunched his face up. "Why are you being such a bitch? Why are you even on this army?"

Becca smirked as she stepped closer towards Caleb. "You really want to know?"

"Yes!"

"Because...I...am from the Ice Kingdom. And I work for Queen Saphielle."

Caleb stumbled backwards. "You're a traitor."

"Indeed I am. The Queen found out King Bartholomew's plans, that bastard! She sent me—oh, and Eve—to your kingdom to *join* the army."

THE KING'S ARMY

Caleb couldn't believe what he was hearing.

"She sent us to join the army and to stop you bunch of tosspots from entering our kingdom and saving the princess. She's *ours* now."

10

CALEB WAS THROWN against the row of barrels lined up against the side of the ship, his sword flying across to the other side of the deck, hitting the floor with a clunk. He groaned in pain, holding onto his sides. Becca stomped over and used lifted him without even touching him before slamming him back down on the deck, face first. Blood spurted from Caleb's nose, splattering across her shoes.

"What a mess!" Becca laughed. "Oh dear."

She lifted him again and threw him against the ship's side, narrowly missing a sword sticking up. Caleb screwed his face up in agony. Pain rippled through his body, almost like he was being stabbed multiple times. The impact of him hitting the wall knocked the breath out of him and he struggled for oxygen. For a few moments, Caleb held onto his chest, focusing on his breathing.

At that moment, the hatch shot open, and Caleb was blinded by the sun beaming straight down into his face. Becca stumbled backwards so not to be caught attacking Caleb.

"Everything okay?" Shayne asked.

Caleb gathered his breath. "No, she —"

THE KING'S ARMY

"Everything is fine," interrupted Becca, "we were just having a mock battle just in case he needs to fight the Queen; see if he has the balls to fight a lady."

"Take it he lost?"

Becca looked down at her bloodied victim.

"Yes." She let out a chuckle and followed Shayne. Becca looked back and squinted her eyes at Caleb, sending a strong message to him.

Caleb knew he couldn't do anything about her. Not yet anyway. The timing needed to be right. He wasn't sure how, but he was determined he would expose Becca for what-for *who*-she was.

⋆

His new surroundings intimidated Caleb. Trees towered over him, icy vines hanging from every branch he could see. The smell of frozen soil filled the air and Caleb breathed it all in. It didn't smell that bad at all — in fact, it was quite calming. That's what he needed right now. After his altercation with Becca, Caleb needed to calm down.

A jungle.

The edge of the canal was frozen solid, but the middle was clear and still liquified. Rocks of all shapes and sizes lined the edges, moss gradually forming across them, spreading like a virus. Branches hung low making the army duck as the ship passed through.

The intimidation of the new surroundings eased, and Caleb managed to calm himself. Small scars

THE KING'S ARMY

covered his face, his nose still sore from his brutal attack. He was secretly planning ways to expose Becca; to get his revenge on her. But he didn't know how he would do it.

Becca was a smooth talker and everyone on the army loved her. What made it even harder was that Eve was *also* from the Ice Kingdom. Becca had threatened to murder the entire army before heading back to her kingdom and killing the princess—so, Caleb had felt the need to stay quiet. If he said anything, no one would be safe from her psychotic behaviour. She was just like the Winter Queen.

Now he thought about it though, it did seem odd that they volunteered for the army in the first place considering the Shihan Kingdom had very few female warriors—and those who were warriors didn't have a lot of training due to the sexist nature of the royals.

"Do you reckon this is it?" a deep voice asked from behind, startling Caleb.

"What?" Caleb said, dazed.

Shayne rolled his eyes. "Is this the Deep South?"

"I don't know. It could be, it certainly *looks* like it could be."

The air grew a little warmer, but it was still crisp. They were heading south; Caleb was sure of it. Up ahead, a sign was secured into the ground. It looked quite fancy, clean, neat. Not like its surroundings. As the ship approached, Caleb carefully read the sign.

Grata ad Meridiem Gurgite: Welcome to the Deep South.

THE KING'S ARMY

"They don't speak English here?" Caleb questioned.

Shayne looked at the sign as the ship drifted across the water, slowly. "Doesn't look like it. The translation but be purely for English-speaking elves. The original text must be the only language they speak here."

Caleb scratched his chin as he thought. "Do you think anyone lives here?"

"We'll soon find out."

The ship exited the jungle and appeared in the middle of an ocean. In the distance stood a lone mountain, covered in snow, and surrounded by a large ice glacier. The ship floated across the ocean, slowly cutting through the emptiness that surrounded the army.

"What's that?" Damien called.

Caleb turned around and spotted Damien pointing towards the mountain. He looked over and saw an opening. He urged the ship to move faster, but of course, it didn't.

"Maybe the princess is in there," said Shayne.

"Maybe she is," interrupted Becca, "maybe she isn't."

"Piss off!" snapped Caleb.

"I beg your pardon?"

"You heard, traitor!"

Everyone went silent. Becca glared at Caleb, her eye twitching, anger building on her face.

"What do you mean?" Damien asked. "How is Becca a traitor?"

THE KING'S ARMY

Caleb struggled to speak. He wanted to tell them. He *had* to tell them. But the words wouldn't leave his mouth. Becca's threats lingered in his mind—he couldn't say anything. He would remain silent.

"Nothing," he finally said, "we were just messing around earlier, playing a game. I lost and I'm quite a sore loser."

Everyone went back to what they were doing. Caleb looked around anxiously, worried that Becca wouldn't stick to her word, regardless of what he did. One minute, he could be alive. The next, he could be dead because Becca decided she couldn't trust him. Caleb cleared his throat, trying to remain calm. Becca wandered over to Eve and they spoke among themselves, looking over at Caleb every few seconds. He couldn't figure out what they were saying, but he knew it was about him.

The ship docked at the edge of the mountains, opposite the cave opening. The army departed the ship and crowded outside the cave. Caleb glared at Becca. If the princess *was* in here, Becca would kill them all to prevent them from taking her home. And then, she would probably kill *her* too.

"Who's going in first?" Shayne asked.

"Becca should," Caleb said. "And Eve. Ladies first."

Caleb knew exactly what he was doing. Send the traitors in first, kill them from behind if there were any signs of trouble.

THE KING'S ARMY

"Why?" Eve said. "Why can't one of you go first? Gentlemen protecting the ladies."

"Thought you were strong women? Why do you need us to protect you?"

Becca cut in front of Eve. "Because it's a man's job to protect a lady."

"No, it's our job as individual living beings that we protect ourselves and our kingdom. All of us, not just the men. Why are you here if you don't want to protect *yourselves*?"

"What has got into you both lately?" Damien asked. "You've been at each other's throats all day."

"She's a traitor," said Caleb.

"Not this again!" Becca yelled, rolling her eyes. "Get over it, Caleb!"

"Over what? The fact you *actually* work for the Winter Queen and aren't part of our kingdom at all?"

Everyone shot a glare at Becca.

Becca scowled at Caleb.

"You shit!" Becca roared. "You shitting shit!"

Becca lunged towards Caleb, wrapping her hands around his throat. She lifted him high in the air and threw him against the snow-covered rocks and watched him slide to the floor. Caleb groaned as pain shot up his spine. For a moment, he felt like he was going to pass out. Nothing could have prepared him for this. Becca stomped over to him and went to grab him again but was pulled back by a strong grip of energy. Caleb gathered himself to his feet but was thrown onto

THE KING'S ARMY

the ice, his weight shattering it and causing him to fall straight through, drenching him in freezing water. Caleb flapped around in the water as he struggled to keep afloat. Becca dived towards him and tightly gripped his neck, pushing his head under the water and holding it there for five seconds at a time. She pulled his head from the water, allowing Caleb to breathe for two seconds before smashing his head into the ice-cold water again. Caleb tried to scream, but he couldn't. Water poured down his throat, filling his lungs.

"Stop it!" screamed Shayne. "Stop it you revolting bitch!"

Caleb jumped back up from underwater as Shayne grabbed Becca by the scruff of her neck and punched her stomach, sending a shot of hot energy through her and causing her to collapse to the ground. Damien helped Caleb from the water and dragged him to the land. Caleb coughed up all the water he had swallowed and lay flat on the ground to catch his breath. He shivered, breathing heavily and his teeth chattering together. But there was nothing to help warm him up. He just had to deal with it.

Eve charged over and positioned her crossbow, ready to aim at Caleb's head. Caleb had no energy to fight back, so he just stayed where he was, expecting to die any second now. But before she could pull the trigger, an arrow shot through her neck, blood splattering all over the snow. She fell to the floor. Dead.

"Shit," said Caleb, shooting up from the ground and looking at Eve's bloodied dead body.

THE KING'S ARMY

Becca stirred and slowly sat upright, holding her stomach. "You'll regret this." She struggled for breath, still affected by Shayne's strong blows to her body. The men laughed at her. Caleb knew her time was almost up. It wouldn't be long before she was dead too. And then, they would be one step closer to saving Princess Kate.

⊙❋⊙

Inside the cave, it was cold. A bitter breeze drifted through, stroking Caleb's face, making his eyes water.

"Dark, isn't it?" said Damien.

"Anyone got a candle?" Caleb asked.

No one did. They would remain in complete darkness. Caleb prayed silently that there wouldn't be any surprise booby-traps in the cave. He also prayed that they were the only ones in there. Caleb ran his right hand along the walls to guide his way through. He advised the army to do the same and slowly edge forward so not to make any abrupt movements that could result in serious injury.

"Good job back there," said Caleb, "you did well."

"She deserved it," replied Damien. "After what she did to you, it was only fair to treat her the same — and worse."

Caleb giggled. "Using your invisibility power on that rock really made all the difference. Oh, and thank you for helping me."

THE KING'S ARMY

"No problem. We're in this together."

Just as Caleb was about to respond, a gentle growl echoed through the cave. A rush of fire blasted out in front of the army from the path on the far right.

"Shit," whispered Caleb, "we're in a dragon's cave."

I I

FIRE BLASTED OUT in front of the army once again, filling the cave with an exasperating heat. Caleb jumped back as the thick flames raced towards him. A gentle growl followed by a furious screech echoed around the cave, startling Caleb, and the army.

"We need to get out of here," whispered Lewis, "this dragon is dangerous."

Caleb shook his head - not that Lewis could see him do this. "We need to find the princess."

"She might not even be in here."

"But that's not a risk we can take. We came here to rescue her; we have to check every nook and cranny of this kingdom."

Shayne placed a hand on Caleb's shoulder. "Are you sure you want to risk your life? We all have powers; you don't."

"Yeah, I don't need to be reminded!" snapped Caleb.

Again, fire blasted out from the right, the heat blowing in everyone's faces.

Caleb lowered his tone. "Look, I'm here for the same reason as everyone else. Yes, I'll have to adjust my fighting tactics, but I *can* do this. And anyway, your powers are going to be weak as shit against this

THE KING'S ARMY

dragon—or drag*ons!* God knows how many dragons are in here."

Nobody moved or spoke for a moment. The dragon had stopped blasting fire from its mouth—although Damien had joked the dragon was firing it from its arse—allowing the army to run through to the next path before they were set alight.

"Should we run through to the tunnel that's up ahead?" Damien whispered.

"On the count of three," Caleb said, "we can run. Make sure you *don't* get caught by the dragon. The winter bitch can't take more of our lives."

"Okay. I'll try not to die." Damien giggled.

Caleb rolled his eyes. "One..."

Caleb tensed his shoulders.

"...two..."

Caleb was riddled with anxiety as sweat dripped down his face.

"...three!"

Everyone ran, zigzagging left to right as fire blasted towards them, flames licking the rocky walls of the cave. Caleb leaped and dived to avoid the flames. He escaped the path of the dragon's fire and got himself to safety in the tunnel in front of him, awaiting everyone else to join him. The scream of one his team rang through his ears, sticking to his mind.

"Shit!" he roared. "Who's on fire?"

Nobody responded.

"I said, *who* is on *fire*?"

"Shayne!" Damien shouted. "Shayne's on fire!"

THE KING'S ARMY

Shayne's on fire.

Those words were glued to his mind. Super-glued.

Shayne's on fire.

No, he couldn't be.

"You're lying!" Caleb cried.

"I'm sorry, Caleb. I'm not lying. I wish I was."

Caleb turned the corner and watched as his brightly lit best friend burned to death. The flames grew higher, engulfing Shayne's body, sucking him into the arms of death.

"No!" Caleb cried, his voice cracking.

※

The army had found another pathway in the cave, taking them to safety away from the dragons. Caleb didn't speak. He couldn't. Only ten minutes ago, he had watched his best friend die. Again, Queen Saphielle had taken another life from the army. He sat against the wall. It wasn't particularly comfortable, but that was the least of his worries right now.

"Are you okay?" Damien asked.

Caleb didn't respond. Instead, he fixated his eyes on the floor. Damien held a torch he had taken from the cave's wall, freshly lit by the dragon's flames and crouched down next to his new friend.

"Caleb."

Caleb looked up at Damien.

"Are you okay?"

THE KING'S ARMY

"Shayne...he's gone," muttered Caleb.

"We'll be okay. Once we've fought that dragon—or dragons—and killed it—or them—this cave will be a bit safer for us."

"My best friend is dead. I don't care about my safety right now."

Damien rubbed Caleb's arm. "Your safety is still important. I understand you're hurting. But honestly, you need to snap out of it whilst we're here. We need to save the princess."

"Sod the princess!" Caleb screamed.

Damien jumped back, startled by Caleb's sudden outburst. Caleb couldn't believe what he had just said. He knew Damien was right—but the grief was too much for him. The trauma of watching Shayne die was sneaking up on him. The image of his best friend's death was engraved in his mind, and it wasn't going anywhere.

"Sorry," Caleb muttered.

"It's okay," said Damien. "Come on. We've got to keep going."

Caleb staggered to his feet and gathered his emotions. He needed to stay strong. The army trudged through the cave, looking around every corner and freezing as soon as they heard even the *slightest* noise.

A gentle growl echoed around.

Caleb froze. "Bollocks."

"Shush," whispered Lewis, "we've got to stay quiet."

THE KING'S ARMY

The army moved slowly, edging towards the corner of the tunnel they had found safety in. Damien stuck his head around and shone the torch. Caleb anxiously swallowed the lump forming in his throat.

"Nothing here," said Damien.

He led the army down the path ahead of them but froze when another growl echoed around them. This time, it was louder than before.

"There's another dragon," said Caleb, "we're going to die."

"No, we're not," said Lewis. "We'll be fine."

"How do you know that?"

"We've got weapons and magic to fight with whatever comes our way."

Caleb sighed. "We should have all stuck together. There's no way we should have split up. Jesse would have been perfect in this situation."

"Thought you didn't like him."

"I didn't. But he's a brilliant fighter. So were Eve and Becca, but they turned out to be lying bitches."

"That's true," said Damien. "But we have to forget about them now. They've gone. Come on."

The army kept on moving, slowly and steadily. Caleb didn't know how he was going to defeat the dragons. With no magic in his system, and just a few members of the army here, it was going to be a challenge.

Growl.

Caleb thought he could hear the direction the growling was coming from. But he wasn't one hundred percent sure.

THE KING'S ARMY

"Guys," he said, "I think it's coming from down here."

Caleb pointed towards a path on his left. Damien shone the torch down the path and saw a black, scaled beast laying in the centre of the path. Its eyes glowed a mustard yellow, red veins creeping down its eyeballs. Caleb glared at its teeth—large, pointy, a dirty brown tint. One bite and it would be fatal.

It growled.

Damien moved his torch away and pushed Caleb and Lewis away from the path. "We need a plan. What are we going to do?"

"Throw the torch down there," Caleb suggested. "Set it on fire."

"And then we won't see where we're going."

"We coped before."

"Shayne didn't!" Lewis spat, cutting in.

Caleb bowed his head.

"Sorry. Look, we need a better plan. We can't set things on fire. And anyway, dragons literally breathe fire so being set on fire probably won't affect them much."

"We can give it a go." Caleb was determined to watch this dragon burn. They killed his best friend, so it was time for him to get revenge.

He snatched the torch from Damien's grip and stormed over to the path where the dragon was resting.

"What are you doing?" Damien snapped.

THE KING'S ARMY

Caleb threw the torch like a javelin and watched as the dragon burst into flames, crackling and popping as the fire rippled across the dragon's scaly skin.

"You dickhead!" Damien roared. "This could be *very* dangerous for us!"

"Oh, shut up!" Caleb shouted. "It's dying."

The dragon continued to crackle and pop. A sudden burst of flames startled Caleb. The fire turned from orange to white and purple. Caleb watched in confusion.

"What the—"

The dragon burst from the flames, doubling in size.

"Oh shit!"

Caleb ran back in the direction they came from. He looked back and noticed Damien and Lewis back away from the path as the dragon emerged. They ran in Caleb's direction.

"Run!" Lewis yelled.

The three ran away from the dragon as it burst through the cave and darted towards them. Lewis and Damien attempted to fight it with their powers, but they weren't strong enough - the dragon overpowered their magic. Caleb couldn't do anything except run. He was useless.

Why did I ever think I could do this?

As the three raced through the cave, dragons emerged from all directions, blocking their path, threatening to hurt and kill them. The dragon that was once on fire burst through the rock walls, smashing them to

THE KING'S ARMY

nothing but debris. It glowed a bright purple as the fire continued to burn.

"Damien, I know you said you can only make objects invisible," said Caleb, "but do you think you could *try* to make us all invisible right now?"

"I can't make elves invisible!" shouted Damien, panting. "No matter how hard I try."

Caleb sighed. "How about making these rocks invisible? If we pile enough of them up tightly and then you hide them, the dragons' path *might* be blocked."

Damien didn't respond. Instead, he drew his sword and pointed it towards one of the dragons. It growled before letting out a frighteningly loud roar. It blew fire from its mouth, hurtling in Caleb's direction. Caleb jumped out of the way, avoiding the flames, and saving himself from the same fate as his best friend.

"Come on then!" Caleb yelled. "Give me your best shot!"

The dragon threw fire from its mouth again. Caleb avoided it and pulled his flail from his belt, swinging it at the dragon, bashing it on the head. Blood slowly leaked from the cut, but not enough to kill it. Seconds later, the incision sealed itself and the dragon was back to normal. The flail wasn't powerful enough to kill dragons. *Shit!*

"What?" Caleb cried. "Die you stupid prick!"

Caleb swung his flail at the dragon again, this time in the leg but it did nothing. But just like before, the dragon survived. It darted towards Caleb, not

THE KING'S ARMY

breathing fire, but instead snarling. Its grim teeth made him want to vomit.

Caleb ran.

The dragon chased.

Caleb didn't know how to outrun this dragon. He could trick it into thinking he was going in one direction, but then actually go another. But it wouldn't be long before the dragon figured it out. So, he decided that idea was out the window.

He picked his pace up but tripped on a stalagmite, sending him across the ground. The dragon towered over him, flapping its wings.

The dragon roared, making Caleb flinch.

Suddenly, its neck flung to one side, and it collapsed to the ground with a loud thump, an arrow sticking out of its head. Caleb stared at it, taking in what had just happened. He looked over and saw Lewis holding a crossbow, still in position as if he was going to shoot it again.

"Did you just—" Caleb couldn't finish his sentence.

"Yep," said Lewis, "now come on, we have to get out of here before the rest of them come."

The cave rumbled around them like an earthquake was occurring. Caleb knew the rest of the dragons were coming. He staggered to his feet and ran with Lewis and Damien. They found the cave's exit and ran straight through it, escaping the cave and heading in the direction of their ship. The cold air hit them hard, and they shivered as they stood on the island, staring at

THE KING'S ARMY

the cave. Dragons scrambled at the cave door but couldn't get out.

Caleb wandered back to the ship and pulled the door down. "Ready to go?"

Lewis and Damien boarded the ship and Caleb followed, before closing the door and securing it shut.

"Well, the princess isn't here," said Caleb. "Shall we explore further or head back to the main Ice Kingdom?"

"I think we should do a little bit more exploring," said Damien, "just to make sure we've looked everywhere."

Caleb made it his duty to captain the ship and he manoeuvred it away from the cave. Once again, they were on the move.

12

THE COLD AIR brushed against Caleb's skin, goosebumps forming all over his body. He wanted to get back to the mainland now. The army needed to be reunited and work as one. Working as two divisions was not working nor was it convenient.

"Should we just head back to The Ice Kingdom?" Caleb asked. "It's clear as day that the princess isn't here."

"No," said Lewis, "we can't give up. Princess Kate could be anywhere—and that includes here. We need to continue exploring further."

"I just think it would be so much easier if the others were here too. Just the three of us isn't at all convenient."

Lewis looked at Damien but didn't say a word—his face said it all.

"Okay," Damien said, "we'll go back, get the others, and come back here."

"Deal."

Caleb began to turn the ship around, headed towards the Ice Kingdom. It began to snow heavily, the fragile snowflakes landing firmly on Caleb's face. The view became an image of white. Nothing else was visible.

THE KING'S ARMY

"I can't see anything!" Caleb shouted.

The top deck was becoming nothing but a large sheet of snow as the storm grew heavier and hit the ship harder and harder. Caleb turned to the others, asking if he should turn back and dock the ship whilst they wait for the snow to stop.

"Just keep going," said Damien, "I'm sure the snow will stop soon."

"It bloody better! Because otherwise we're going to have to dock somewhere and sit in the lower deck until the storm passes," Caleb said.

The snowstorm showed no sign of stopping any time soon, and Caleb made the decision to dock the ship on the edge of the mountains. The army headed down to the lower deck and closed the hatch to stop the snow from filling the ship even more.

"We're not getting out of here any time soon, are we?" asked Lewis.

"Doesn't look like it," said Damien. "Caleb made the right decision — we had to stop the journey."

Caleb laid back, resting his head on a barrel. "The ocean will be frozen. We're gonna be stuck."

"Don't worry, it will be fine."

Caleb sighed and closed his eyes. He just wanted to sleep. Today had been a long day. Losing Shayne had taken a serious toll on his mental health. All he wanted to do was forget.

THE KING'S ARMY

It was dark by the time the snowstorm had stopped. And now, their voyage was even more dangerous. The warriors of the Ice Kingdom had an advantage. Caleb prayed that he and his friends made it back safely, and that it would be easy to locate the other army recruits.

The ship rocked from side to side as the wind pushed the waves across the ocean, knocking the ship in all directions. Caleb gripped the ship's steering wheel, keeping it under control as the waves grew stronger.

"Stormy one tonight," said Lewis. "We need to be extra careful."

"Don't worry," replied Caleb, "Damien is on guard, so he'll let us know if there is anyone or anything around."

Caleb looked up, the half-moon glistening in the night sky, surrounded by stars dotted around like the freckles on his sister's face. He smiled. Despite how dangerous this kingdom was, he couldn't help but find peace in the night sky.

His peace didn't last long. A large black object covered the moon, plunging the sky into complete darkness. Caleb furrowed his brow—that was until he saw the fire. The dragons were back and ready to attack the army.

"Shit," said Caleb, "we need to get to safety."

"Why?" Damien asked.

"The dragons. They're back."

Damien looked up. "Shit."

THE KING'S ARMY

Caleb let go of the steering wheel now that the waves on the ocean had calmed down. He grabbed his crossbow and gripped it tightly, ready to shoot when he saw a dragon come near. Lewis and Damien had their swords, not that they would be any use.

"Dragon!" Caleb cried.

He shot the crossbow and the arrow hit the dragon directly in the eye, blood shooting from its body and the beast fell into the ocean with an almighty splash. The impact rocked the ship, but Caleb quickly grabbed the steering wheel and got the ship back under control.

A swarm of dragons hovered overhead, moving in a circular motion like they were in a cult. Caleb knew he was going to need more than just his crossbow to fight these dragons. His flail wouldn't be any use, and his sword would be useless too. The only thing he felt he needed right now was magic.

One dragon dived towards the ship. Caleb steered the ship away from it, preventing the fire from the beast's mouth setting the ship alight. More dragons swooped down from the sky, aiming straight for the ship.

Caleb shot his crossbow, the arrow narrowly missing the dragon's wing. "Bollocks."

He fired another arrow, this time striking the dragon's neck. For a few seconds, the dragon spasmed in the sky before dropping, landing on the deck of the ship with a crash.

THE KING'S ARMY

"What are we meant to do with that?" shrieked Lewis.

"Don't worry about that for now," said Caleb, "we've got to get rid of this lot too!"

Caleb kept firing his crossbow, each arrow missing each dragon. He very quickly ran out of arrows. Damien and Lewis attempted to use their weapons, but they were nowhere near as useful as the crossbow. Caleb raced down the steps to the lower deck and grabbed a flail. It was now that he didn't have any other option. The flail was his last chance. Gripping the weapon tightly, he rushed back to the top deck and waited for a dragon to dive towards him.

"Guys, stand back," said Caleb.

He waited for Damien and Lewis to take a few steps back before he started swinging his flail around. A dragon flapped its wings profusely, darting towards Caleb. As soon as it came near, Caleb directed his swinging flail at its head, knocking it straight into the ocean. Blood splattered over the side of the ship.

"Shit," said Lewis, "you're good!"

Caleb couldn't believe it. Finally, someone had faith in him. No one had ever said 'you're good' to him before. Without magic, Caleb knew he had a disadvantage against the dragons but so far, he was successful. Lewis' words meant the world to him. He didn't know how he had managed to perfect his skills, but he was proud of himself for learning so quickly.

Damien and Lewis ran down the steps to the lower deck, leaving Caleb on his own. Caleb kept

THE KING'S ARMY

swinging his flail every time a dragon came near. Sometimes, he missed, and the dragon would swiftly get ready to attack again. Other times, he knocked the dragon straight across the head, smashing it to the ground.

"Caleb!" called Damien.

Caleb turned his head and saw Damien and Lewis standing by the ship's mast, preparing to climb.

"You stay low," said Lewis, "we'll climb up and try to get the dragons from up here."

Damien and Lewis stood proudly, their bow and arrows securely attached to their uniforms. They nodded at Caleb before turning to climb up the mast. Caleb focused his attention on the task at hand. Dragons were still flying around above him, not showing any sign of leaving. He made the decision to keep the ship moving. If he didn't, they'd be stuck here for days.

✤

The ship smashed against the waves as it re-entered the Ice Kingdom. There was still a long way to go before the army arrived back at the central island, but Caleb didn't mind. They were out of the Deep South; that was all he cared about.

"Do you think we'll be safe from here?" Damien asked.

"I doubt it," said Caleb, "this place is covered from top to bottom."

THE KING'S ARMY

"True. I haven't seen any dragons for a while though, maybe they're asleep."

Caleb sighed. He didn't believe the dragons would be sleeping while their home was being invaded by the opposing kingdom. Instead, he thought they'd be flying around, preparing to attack and kill anything that got in their way or proved a danger to their habitat.

"Let's just get back to the central island," said Caleb. "We need to get the others."

Stars twinkled above; the ocean had calmed, and the journey was smoother now, so Caleb found it easier to control the ship. He hadn't found it this easy since the voyage began yesterday morning. He looked into the water and saw a shadow suddenly jump out between the waves and back in again, causing a loud, big splash and pouring water over the side of the ship.

"What was that?" Lewis asked, startled by the splash.

"Probably just a water dragon," replied Caleb. "They're usually harmless."

"How do you know?"

"My mother told me about them. She had this book—my father's diary. He wrote in it every day up until his death when he was at war. He briefly mentioned water dragons, and he said they were the most harmless breed of dragon. My mum showed it to me when I turned sixteen and read some of it out to me."

Caleb fell silent, reminiscing about his father's tales. His father's diary was less of a journal and more of a memoir about his time in the war, and the day-to-

THE KING'S ARMY

day happenings. The water dragons were a minor detail, a passing observation his father had documented. It was mere trivia for Caleb, until now. Something he never thought he would encounter. He silently prayed that his father was right. The last thing he needed was for more battles against dragons.

"So, we're definitely safe from them, yeah?" Lewis asked, desperate for reassurance.

Caleb nodded. "Yes, we're safe. Unless the Winter Bitch has trained these ones to be brutal little shits too."

"Nothing surprises me about this place."

Caleb continued to sail the ship across the ocean. Although it was dark, he could just about make out the mountains in the distance. The moon sat behind the cluster of mountains, stars decorating the sky. It was a gorgeous view and for a moment, Caleb forgot where he was. Instead, he just admired the view. That was until he started feeling slightly faint.

"Can one of you two take over this for a bit?" Caleb asked, feeling drowsy. His eyes were heavy, and his head was pounding, a strong pain smashing against his temples.

"Sure." Damien stood up and jogged over to the steering wheel.

Caleb sat down and closed his eyes. He was exhausted. Since arriving at the Ice Kingdom, he hadn't slept. He was too scared to. If he went to sleep, he might never wake up.

THE KING'S ARMY

"I think we should dock at the nearest docking port and get some sleep. We'll need our energy for tomorrow," Lewis suggested.

"No!" Caleb snapped. "We can't sleep. If we do, they have an advantage."

"Mate, calm down. There are battle rules for a reason. Warriors have the right to rest at night. No battle is allowed to happen between the hours of 9pm and 8am."

"And how do we know what time it is?"

Lewis went down to the lower deck and came back a few minutes later with a pocket watch. "The king gave us this."

Caleb took it from Lewis's hand and stared at it. The thin hand ticked around, one click at a time.

Tick, tock. Tick, tock. Tick, tock.

Time was passing by slowly. It was only 11pm.

Caleb was still adamant to go to sleep. He feared the Ice Kingdom warriors and dragons would attack whilst he rested. He was scared he wouldn't wake up.

⚜

The wolves charged towards him, baring their teeth. Caleb ran in the opposite direction, escaping the wolves' path. They were approaching him quickly, drool dripping from their mouths. Each wolf growled and barked at him. Caleb looked away from them and continued to run.

"Help!" Caleb screamed.

THE KING'S ARMY

He didn't have any weapons with him, so he couldn't even try to fight back. The only option he had was to keep running and hope he would find somewhere safe to hide. Above, dragons hovered, but they showed no sign of causing him harm. But Caleb knew it wouldn't be too long before they started to attack once they spotted the wolves charging after him.

"Somebody help!" Caleb cried out. "Please, somebody help!"

Caleb looked over his shoulder. The wolves were still chasing him, teeth bared and heavy growls coming from their throats. He turned back around so he didn't have to watch the wolves, but he was greeted by a slim woman. Caleb skidded to a halt, his heart hammering against his chest. The woman in front of him didn't look familiar. She had long, curly black hair. Her dark blue eyes shot straight through him as if she were setting a curse upon him. Her black lipstick told Caleb everything he needed to know — this woman was a real *bitch*. The woman held a sceptre, topped with a ball of ice. A crown sat gently on her rough, ragged hair. It took Caleb a moment, but then he realised who he had been confronted by.

The Winter Queen.

"Hello, Caleb," she said.

Caleb looked behind him. The wolves had stopped, but they were surrounding him, still baring their teeth. They were ready to attack.

"Greetings, Your Majesty," said Caleb, bowing to the monarch.

THE KING'S ARMY

"Playing kiss-chase with my little friends?"

Caleb giggled nervously. "No, no...er...they were chasing me for no reason."

"For no reason?"

"I don't know what reason they had to be chasing me. It just...happened."

The Winter Queen stared at Caleb, squinting her eyes, her soulless stare piercing through Caleb. He looked away awkwardly, the queen's presence causing him a great discomfort.

"You realise you're trespassing, right?" the Winter Queen said.

"Trespassing?" Caleb laughed. "You've abducted royalty!"

"I *am* royalty, I can do what I want. And anyway, it's hardly abduction when—"

◊

Caleb jolted awake. Lewis was gripping his shoulder and shaking him hard.

"Wake up!" Lewis shouted. "We're back in the Ice Kingdom."

It took Caleb a moment to properly become aware of his surroundings. He was sure he was already here. "The wolves..."

"What?" Damien asked.

"The wolves. They were chasing me. And the Winter Queen, she was here as well."

THE KING'S ARMY

"It was just a dream," said Lewis. "You've been asleep for hours. It's 6am. Almost time to battle."

Caleb shook his head. "I can't, I don't have enough energy."

Lewis handed him an energy bar made from oats and chocolate. "Eat this. King Bartholomew left loads in a box downstairs. These have to last us the entire battle, so don't be greedy."

Caleb took the energy bar from Lewis and bit into it. Eating straight away after waking up didn't compliment his stomach very well, but he dealt with it. He needed energy. Today was an important day—another day of battle. But he wasn't ready for any of it. His dream had really put him down, put a lot of fear into him. Would the wolves really chase him like they did in his dream?

Caleb stood up and wandered to the edge of the ship. He looked around. The same mountains from before. The same trees and bushes. It was quiet. *So* quiet that Caleb didn't believe that no one was around. Somewhere, somebody had to be hiding, ready to attack. Although, like Lewis said, it was only 6am. Battles can't start until 8am. So that put Caleb's mind at rest—kind of. He didn't know what the elves here were like. For all he knew, they could be rule breakers and attack at any given chance they get.

"What are we supposed to do for two hours then?" Caleb asked.

THE KING'S ARMY

"We explore the land," said Damien, "we find somewhere to hide and prepare for battle. We need to be somewhere safe, somewhere they can't find us."

"Good luck with that, it's like they have eyes everywhere."

Damien nodded. "That's a good point. We just have to be careful. But we can't stay here for two hours. That's not productive."

"So, what do we do?" Caleb groaned. "Once we've found somewhere to hide, what do we do in there?"

"Prepare for battle," Damien explained. "We practice using our weapons. Practice makes perfect and that's the only way we'll succeed."

The threesome went down to the lower deck and browsed the selection of weapons. Caleb chose a bow and arrow, and a flail - both great weapons for different needs. Lewis and Damien both chose a sword. They left the ship and wandered through the land, hunting for somewhere to stay. They stayed low so no one could see them, but they remained cautious. Queen Saphielle could see everything—she would know where they were and could easily send her army out to kill them.

Snow gently floated from the sky, the air growing colder and colder. The Ice Kingdom was a land of nothing. It was very underwhelming considering it was one of the wealthiest kingdoms in the realm. All Caleb could see up ahead was mountains and trees, more mountains, and more trees. He didn't know how far the kingdom ran. It could be huge; it could be small. The

THE KING'S ARMY

army crawled along the ground, the coldness sticking to Caleb's body. He shivered but kept moving—he couldn't stop now.

Suddenly, a clomp of footsteps vibrated around them. Caleb took some deep breaths, anxiety firing through him. He knew he needed to pull himself together; he couldn't be feeling like this in battle. The three jumped behind a bush. Caleb poked his head over the top. Nearby, a squad of guards marched through the kingdom, holding their swords high. Caleb squatted back behind the bush and turned to Damien and Lewis.

"Guards," he whispered. "There's a whole squad."

"Shit," said Lewis, "do you think they're going to try and start the battle earlier than they're allowed to?"

"God knows what they're like here. I don't trust them; we need to stay low and get to somewhere safe."

"Nowhere is safe."

"You know what I mean."

The three picked their weapons up and gripped them tightly, before crawling through the snow. Caleb winced as his hands froze in the cold. He stopped every few seconds to rub his hands together in an attempt to warm them up, but he decided there wasn't much point him doing that as he would be digging his hands into the snow again and again until there was somewhere safe for him and the army to hide.

THE KING'S ARMY

"Do you think we'll find the others?" Caleb whispered.

"I'm sure we will," replied Damien.

"They could be anywhere. It's going to take ages."

"It might not."

Caleb pushed his hands into the snow and felt something crunch underneath him.

"Hold on a second," he called out.

Damien and Lewis stopped and turned around, looking at Caleb.

"What is it?" Damien asked.

Caleb stared at the spot where he felt the crunch. "There's something here. I felt and heard it."

"Is it really the best idea to look at what it could be though? It could be a trap."

Caleb started flicking the snow away, sending flakes flying everywhere, some landing on Lewis's clothing.

And there it was.

A brown sheet of paper laid perfectly still, secured by the weight of the snow on its edges. It looked ancient. It took Caleb a moment to realise he was looking at a map—a map of the Ice Kingdom.

"Oh my God!" Caleb exclaimed, excitedly. "It's a map."

"A map?" Lewis echoed.

"Yes, a map."

He pulled it from the ground and shook the snow off it. Small sketches covered the map, each

THE KING'S ARMY

indicating what was located where. Mountains surrounded the map—*obviously*. A small circle of buildings was drawn in the centre and were labelled *Deervale Village*. Caleb wondered if this was where the rest of the army could have ended up. A palace sat in the top right of the map - the Winter Queen's palace.

"We're miles away from the palace," announced Caleb. "We're in the south. The palace is in the Northeast."

"Do you think the princess could be there after all?" Damien asked.

"I think she could be. The Deep South had nothing, so she definitely isn't there. The palace has got to be the only place she could be. I doubt the Winter Bitch is stupid enough to hold her hostage in a public area."

Lewis took the map from Caleb's grip and looked at it. "I reckon we could plan a route using this map. It doesn't look like it could take too long."

"Not too long? Lewis, it's miles away!" Caleb screeched. "It's going to take hours, maybe even *days*, to get there."

"Oh, calm down. We start from here, go past the Royal Barracks, through Deervale Village, through the valleys, and up to the palace."

"And what about the warriors, the guards, the dragons, the wolves, and God knows what else along the way?"

"We deal with it. That's what we're here for. If you're going to whinge about fighting, why did you join the army?"

THE KING'S ARMY

Caleb grunted and looked around him. It was clear. "If we move quickly, we can get ourselves to the hut over there." Caleb pointed to a grubby looking hut in the not-too-far distance.

"Go!" Damien yelled.

The threesome ran towards the hut, their weapons ready to wield at any given moment. Luckily for them, they arrived at the hut safely and secured the door shut. Caleb bolted it and crouched below a window.

"Now what?" he asked. "This hut is tiny so we can't prepare for battle."

"Then we discuss our plan. And we discuss how we're going to use the map to our advantage," said Damien.

13

LEWIS PULLED THE pocket watch from his trouser pocket. It was one minute until 8am. The battle was due to start imminently, and they still hadn't found any of the others.

"We desperately need to find the others," said Caleb, "we can't do this without them."

"Don't panic," said Lewis. "We will find them."

The roars of dragons came from outdoors. They were muffled but were clear enough for Caleb to identify them.

"Bollocks," said Caleb, "it's begun."

Lewis slowly rose and briefly looked out the window. He was quiet for a few minutes, but then he crouched back down and turned to Caleb and Damien.

"We're surrounded," he said.

"What are we going to do?" Damien asked.

Caleb thought for a moment. He gently pulled the window across so there was just a small opening. Positioning the bow and arrow, Caleb licked his lips in concentration. And without a second thought, he fired the arrow and watched it penetrate a warrior's neck, blood squirting out. The warrior collapsed to the floor, not moving a muscle. Caleb threw himself onto the

THE KING'S ARMY

floor as the other warrior's charged through the land, looking for where the arrow came from.

"What happened?" Lewis whispered.

"I killed a warrior," said Caleb, proudly.

"Nice one."

The three fell silent so not to be heard. There wasn't much they could do at the moment, especially Caleb. Damien and Lewis had an advantage—they could use their magic. Caleb didn't have that luxury.

"We really need to get out there," said Damien, "otherwise we're going to be stuck here forever."

"Bit of an exaggeration," laughed Caleb.

"Not really. We're surrounded and I doubt they're going to go anywhere any time soon. We just have to get out there and run."

It took a few minutes, but Caleb finally agreed. To start with, they stayed low. Caleb pushed the door open carefully and stepped out. He jumped behind a tree and looked over his shoulder. In the distance stood a squad of guards and their wolves. Caleb knew it was risky, but he agreed with Damien. They had to get out there; there was a princess to save.

Damien and Lewis each jumped behind a bush and looked out for enemies. Caleb took one last look over his shoulder. A wolf was prowling towards him.

"Shit!" exclaimed Caleb.

He grabbed his bow and arrow and shot the wolf with it.

It still breathed, no sign of it dying.

THE KING'S ARMY

"Finish the job," said Lewis, "this wolf could easily be fixed up and be ready to attack again."

Caleb drew his sword. He stared down at the wolf for a few seconds before making his decision. With all his built-up anger and strength, he lifted the sword up high and brought it down again, pushing it straight through the wolf's head. The crunch of its skull rang in Caleb's ears, and blood dripped from the hole created by the sword. As the blood poured from the wolf's head, the snow turned a horrid shade of red.

"Good job," said Damien. "You're actually a good warrior."

"Am I?" Caleb muttered.

"Yes, you are. Maybe you don't have magic, but that isn't the be all and end all. You have a gift of fighting. You were *born* to do this."

Caleb smiled. He still felt like a bad warrior, but hearing Damien's words gave him more confidence. Pride welled within him and for a moment, he remembered why he was here.

"Invaders!" a deep voice yelled.

Caleb came back to reality and poked his head around the tree, panicking as the guards raced towards him, Damien, and Lewis.

"Run!" Caleb screamed.

The three took off, racing through the Ice Kingdom. Arrows fired past them, landing violently in the snow. Some had fire on them, putting them all at an increased risk. Flames burst through the snow, causing

THE KING'S ARMY

the ice underneath to crack slightly. The three army warriors kept running, not daring to look back.

Damien pulled his crossbow from his back and shot an arrow towards the guards. He used his eyes to make the arrow transparent and watched proudly as a guard hit the ground. Again, he fired an arrow, made it invisible, and watched each guard and wolf he hit fall to their potential deaths.

"Shit, that was good!" Caleb shouted. "How'd you do that?"

"Magic," said Damien.

"Of course."

They kept running. Caleb looked over his shoulder and watched the guards struggle to their feet. *Shit, they're still alive.* He turned back around and ran into someone, crashing to the ground.

"Ouch."

Caleb got up and looked down. He'd crashed into Matilda.

"I'm so sorry," said Caleb, offering a hand to help Matilda up. "Are you okay?"

Matilda nodded, brushing the snow off her dress. "I'm fine. Are you okay?"

"I'm fine."

"Really?" Matilda pointed to Caleb's arm. "You don't look it."

Caleb looked down and saw his blood-stained armour. "Shit."

Matilda took his arm and looked at it. "That's going to need healing. Come with me."

THE KING'S ARMY

Caleb was reluctant to leave. He looked over Matilda's shoulder and saw his two friends running. They'd be fine, he needed his injury to be fixed.

Matilda guided Caleb to a small cave at the edge of the kingdom. It was dark at first, but light soon came to be. Torches were secured to the walls, flames flickering and spreading the light all around. There wasn't much in the cave at first, but Caleb soon noticed the basic décor Matilda had displayed around the place. She had made it very homely.

"This is where you live?" asked Caleb.

"No," said Matilda, "this is where I *work*. Sometimes."

Caleb held his arm where he was wounded to stem the bleed. "Must be nice. Seems peaceful."

"It is very peaceful. The rocky walls block out most of the sound from outside-" Matilda pointed to a small, wicker chair at the edge of the cave, inviting Caleb to sit down— "so it means I can work in peace and don't have to worry about being disrupted."

Caleb sat in the chair and watched Matilda gather her concoctions and potions. They were all lined up on numerous shelves on a home-made wooden shelving unit. Each one had its own colour—and each colour had its own row. She looked so beautiful. Caleb looked away before she realised that he was watching her.

"What were you doing out there when it is incredibly dangerous?" asked Caleb.

THE KING'S ARMY

"It's okay," replied Matilda, "they know I'm the healer. The Queen would kill them if they ever hurt me."

"Does she know you're out in the middle of battle?"

"Of course, she does. I'm a healer, it's my job to heal. I'm not going to know if someone needs healing if I'm stuck in here or stuck at the palace all day."

Caleb winced as Matilda dabbed his wound with a cotton wool ball. "You live in the palace?"

"Yeah. Didn't I mention it before?"

"I don't know, can't remember. So much has happened recently that I don't know anything anymore."

Matilda grabbed her yellow potion and poured a small amount on another cotton wool ball. "Where are the rest of your army squad?" She dabbed the wool on Caleb's wound, and he winced as the potion spread through his blood.

"God knows," Caleb said, "they kept running."

"They kept running?"

"Matilda, our princess has been abducted by your Queen. They had no choice; she needs to be rescued."

"I'm sorry, I didn't mean to sound so judgemental."

Matilda took the cotton wool ball away from Caleb's wound and threw it in a bin. She held her hands over the wound and closed her eyes. Caleb closed his eyes too as Matilda began to mutter words under her

THE KING'S ARMY

breath. He couldn't make out what she was saying but he imagined it was some kind of spell—or knowing his luck, a curse.

"What were you saying?" Caleb asked when Matilda pulled away from his arm and stopped muttering.

"I was doing my healing spell," said Matilda. "Your arm should start to heal in no time at all. I can't guarantee a timescale, but I can't imagine it will take too long."

"Thank you."

Matilda smiled. "What are you thanking me for?"

Caleb didn't say anything. Instead, he just stared at her.

That smile.

Matilda's face glowed when she smiled, like a sunny day. Her eyes gleamed as the fire flickered in her pupils. Caleb still didn't say anything. He could sit there all day and admire her beauty. Matilda's face looked so smooth and clean. Caleb clenched his hand into a fist, resisting the temptation to reach out and touch it.

"Everything okay?" Matilda asked.

Caleb snapped out of his daydream. "No, not really."

"What's the matter?"

"Can I kiss you?" Caleb asked abruptly.

"What?" Matilda let out a nervous giggle, her face blushing.

THE KING'S ARMY

"I really want to kiss you. You're so beautiful and I've never met anyone as beautiful as you."

"Caleb—"

"Matilda, I mean it. If I save the princess, I'll have to marry her. I don't want to marry her; I don't have *any* interest in her. But I need to marry her so my family can have a brighter future. This is my last chance to be with someone who I *really* fancy."

Matilda didn't say anything. She smiled nervously and looked away, still blushing. They both fell silent for a few minutes. Caleb knew he had made things awkward. But he couldn't help it, and he wasn't any good at this kind of thing.

Why did I have to say it like that? 'Can I kiss you?' Seriously, what was I thinking?

"I'm sorry," said Caleb. "I didn't mean to freak you out. I'm not very good at this."

"Not very good at what? Kissing?" Matilda teased.

"No." Caleb laughed. "I'm not very good at flirting."

"So, you *are* good at kissing?"

Caleb didn't know what to say. Matilda smirked.

"I didn't say that," said Caleb.

Matilda sighed. "So, you're *not* good at kissing?"

Caleb leaned forward and pressed his lips against Matilda's. He didn't give it a second thought. Everything stopped.

14

FIRE LIT UP the grey sky, dragons flying in all directions. Some of the dragons had an elf sitting on its back, directing it where to go. Caleb ran through the land and jumped behind a rock or a bush every time he was close to danger. He didn't have a clue where the rest of the army were. Damien and Lewis could have reunited with the others and were battling, they could have been imprisoned - Caleb thought back to his dream — or abducted by the Winter Queen.

Caleb fell into a state of panic and ran again, racing through the land, firing arrows at anything that came his way. At this point, he had killed five wolves and one elf. Abruptly, a burst of energy pushed him against a wall, sending his weapons flying across the ground, holding him in place. He fought against it, but he couldn't move. The energy was too strong for him.

"Help!" Caleb yelled, tensing against the strength of the energy.

"There's nowhere for you to run now," said a deep voice.

Caleb opened his tensed eyes and saw a large, muscular elf standing over him. "Who are you?"

The elf laughed. "Conrad. I'm one of the Queen's Guards, your worst nightmare."

THE KING'S ARMY

"Oh yeah?"

"Yeah! I know who you are, how not normal you are. I have an advantage over you and there's nothing you can do about it."

The energy was still pushing against Caleb. His chest began to tighten, his breathing become shallower.

"Please," spluttered Caleb, "let me go."

"And why should I do that?" Conrad asked.

"Because I have a family."

Conrad let out a bellowing laugh. "Do you really think I care?"

The energy grew stronger, and Caleb dug his nails into the rocks. It was painful but it distracted him from the pain this elf was causing him with his magic.

"Please! Can't we battle like normal elves?" Caleb pleaded.

"Normal elves?" Conrad laughed again. "I *am* a normal elf! You're not!"

Caleb kept pushing against the energy. It was too strong, there was no way he was going to be able to set himself free. But he didn't give up; he kept pushing and pushing.

"You may as well give up," said Conrad, "because there is no way you're going to be able to push the energy away from you."

"Why are you doing this?" Caleb asked.

"Because I know what you're here for. I know *who* you're here for. And there is no way I'm letting you get to her."

"You know where she is?"

THE KING'S ARMY

"Of course, I do! I work for the Queen."

"Tell me where she is, you twat!"

Conrad laughed. "You really think calling me a twat is going to make me tell you where your precious little princess is?"

"She's not *my* precious little princess. But she is an important asset to my kingdom and without her, the whole kingdom could fall apart."

"And why's that?" Conrad asked, leaning in closer towards Caleb's face.

"Like I'm going to tell you. Now, let me go!"

Caleb pushed against the energy. The energy weakened and sent Caleb plummeting to the ground. Conrad let out a loud laugh, before becoming serious and drawing his sword.

"You want to battle?" Conrad said. "Well, you've got one. Come on, give me your best shot."

Caleb scowled, thinking about his next move. On one hand, he wanted to fight this bastard and kill him. On the other hand, he wanted to run. He wanted to run as fast and as far as he could. But he figured that running away wouldn't solve anything. Conrad would still be alive, threatening to kill the others.

Caleb drew his sword and held it out in front of him. He and Conrad circled around each other, preparing for battle. Caleb squinted his eyes, his only focus being the murder of his enemy. Conrad smirked, confident he was going to win this battle. He took the first swipe with his blade. Caleb avoided it and watched the

THE KING'S ARMY

elf's weapon cut through the snow, sending the snowflakes flying past him.

"That all you got?" Caleb said. He pounced on the ground, swiped his flail from the snow and swung it at Conrad. It avoided Conrad's body, but it *did* hit the sword in his hand.

Conrad managed to keep a grip on his sword and didn't let go. "Nice try." Again, he swiped his sword at Caleb, catching his arm and drawing a long gash along his bicep.

Caleb winced in pain but didn't scream. He didn't have time for screaming or feeling pain. He needed to *fight*. As he swung his weapon at Conrad, the sky above him became an insult to his ears. Loud screams and roars of dragons pierced his eardrums, fire spraying out of their mouths and lighting up the sky.

"Shit," said Caleb.

He looked at Conrad who was still confidently smirking. Conrad's cocky attitude made Caleb angry — he knew how good Conrad was at fighting. It was obvious. This was his one chance to show that magic can't save everyone all the time. Caleb looked around him and spotted his bow and arrow laying in the snow. He ran to it, swiped it up hastily, dropped his flail, and aimed the arrow at Conrad, holding it in place.

"What you gonna do?" laughed Conrad. "Shoot me?"

Caleb didn't respond. Instead, he positioned the arrow, lowering it towards Conrad's neck. Without warning, Caleb shot the arrow and watched it fly

THE KING'S ARMY

towards Conrad. A ball of energy rumbled and pushed the arrow away from Conrad's direction, it dropping to the ground. Caleb was thrown back and landed on his backside.

"You prick!" Caleb shouted.

Conrad laughed, not caring about Caleb's insults. He lifted his sword and swiped it at Caleb. Caleb rolled out the way and avoided the blow. Instead, the ground took the hit. He drew his sword again and swiped it at Conrad, slicing his leg. Conrad fell to the ground.

"No one beats me!" Conrad growled.

Conrad struggled to his feet and darted towards Caleb. Caleb ran out of the way, but Conrad used his powers to stop him. The energy pushed Caleb to the ground, face first. Caleb rolled over, looking up at the sky. Conrad stood over him, his hairy fat face blocking the view.

"Your time's up," said Conrad.

He drew his sword, raised it above his head, and swung it down towards Caleb's head. Caleb closed his eyes, not wanting to witness his final moments.

Splat.

Caleb didn't open his eyes for a couple of seconds. *Am I alive?*

He opened one eye and noticed Conrad was no longer above him. Caleb opened his other eye and looked to his left.

And there he was.

Conrad.

THE KING'S ARMY

Dead.

"You're welcome," a voice said.

Caleb sat up and saw the entire army stood in front of him. Relief swam through his veins, the tension in his shoulder easing, and despite his history with the army, he couldn't help but smile. "You all found each other then."

"Of course, we did," said Jesse. "And then we came back to find *you*."

"Have you been here all this time?" Lewis asked. "Sorry we left you behind."

"It's all good," said Caleb. "The healer took me to her cave and healed my wounds."

"Did she heal anything else too?" Damien joked. Caleb didn't respond but instead, he smiled, embarrassed.

"Oh my God, you didn't!"

"What's this?" Henry asked.

Caleb had forgotten that not all the army knew he and Matilda had spoken a lot before.

"Caleb fancies the pants off the healer," said Lewis.

"Quite literally by the sounds of it," Jesse replied.

Everyone fell into fits of giggles at the expense of Caleb.

"We need to get out of here," said Caleb, "otherwise we're going to be caught."

The army ran over to the mountains and up the stairway, leading them to the winter forest. It was quiet

THE KING'S ARMY

in the forest, too quiet for Caleb's liking. He knew that somewhere in this forest, there would be a trap—or numerous traps. The army crept quietly, trying not to make any sudden sounds or movements. Twigs that had fallen from trees sat on the pathway. Caleb instructed the army to jump over or walk around them.

"I think the village is on the other side of this woods," whispered Caleb. "As soon as we get there, we know we're one step closer to rescuing the princess."

"How far do you think it is?" Jesse asked.

"Lewis, have you got the map?"

Lewis fumbled around in his pockets and pulled out the map. He handed it to Caleb and watched as Caleb studied it.

"We're probably about two miles from the village," said Caleb.

"How long will it take to get there?" Tobias approached Caleb and looked at the map too.

"Not sure, probably about half an hour? Remember, it will probably take longer though as there are definitely going to be wolves and warriors hiding in this forest. There's no way we're safe."

Everyone looked around.

Silence.

A small bird flew from a tree and out into the open sky. Caleb smiled. Considering the danger this kingdom held, it did have some beautiful nature. The army marched through the forest, their weapons at the ready. Caleb kept looking all around him, making sure he was prepared to fight back at any given moment.

THE KING'S ARMY

An arrow shot down at him, landing just a few feet from him.

"Everyone get ready!" Caleb roared.

Caleb looked up and spotted an Ice Kingdom warrior camouflaged up a tree. He fired one his arrows, hitting the assailant in the face. The elf fell from the tree, screaming in pain.

The King's Army ran through the forest, battling with every elf that made an appearance. Caleb watched as Jesse fought with a short, fat elf. An elf approached him from behind, but Caleb managed to react quickly. He swung his sword at the attacker, but he dodged it. Caleb turned around and the elf was in front of him, avoiding every swipe of his sword. The assailant's supersonic speed was too much for Caleb to handle.

Caleb and the elf fought with their swords, the metal scraping together. Caleb jabbed his sword at the elf, who avoided it again.

"Stop moving!" Caleb boomed. "Using your magic to avoid conflict is a sign of cowardice."

"Oh, do shut up!" the elf spat.

Caleb was pushed to the ground, a sword rising above him. A dragon crashed through the trees, landing on its perch. Caleb jumped to his feet and ran over to the dragon, taunting it, trying to get it to spit out some fire.

"Come on you little shit," said Caleb. "Do your thing."

The dragon glared at Caleb.

THE KING'S ARMY

Caleb swung his sword in front of the dragon's face. The dragon immediately spat out its fire. Caleb caught it on a thick branch that had fallen from a tree and launched it into the middle of the forest. The fire spread quickly, the elves from the Ice Kingdom running frantically away.

Caleb found his squad and they ran, escaping the fire and the elves. He looked back, watching the enemies burn to their deaths.

"That's karma for killing my best friend!" Caleb screamed.

"When did you get so good at fighting?" Jesse asked.

Caleb smiled. "It just came naturally to me. I suppose I took my father's genes. This just proves you don't need magic to fight. You just have to think tactically."

Jesse slapped Caleb on the back. "Good job."

15

THE END OF the forest was near.

Behind the army, the fire was rapidly rising and racing towards them. Caleb was beginning to lose energy and lagged behind. He stopped for a few seconds to catch his breath, but he knew he needed to start running again when the fire rolled towards him.

"Caleb, come on!" Lewis yelled.

Caleb watched as the fire approached nearer. Then, he burst into a sprint, escaping the fire's path and joined the others again. They were so close to the end of the forest.

"We're almost there," announced Jesse. "Come on, we can do this."

Snow began to fall heavily, causing the path to become slippery very quickly. Caleb lost his balance and fell to the ground, sliding a few feet before crashing into a tree. Along his way, he took out some of the others.

"We need to be quicker!" Damien shouted. "The fire is approaching!"

Caleb, Henry, Tobias, and Lewis got up and ran ahead. The others followed.

THE KING'S ARMY

In the distance, Caleb could see a crowd of elves, roaming around the snowy ground, walking in and out of buildings.

The village. Finally.

Within a few minutes, the army were out of the forest and marched through the village. Caleb looked around him. Female elves in pretty dresses, male elves in ragged clothes. It looked just like his home village — except he knew the elves here weren't friendly. The village ran for miles. Caleb couldn't believe the size of it. Small huts sat in rows either side of him, elves wandering in and out, some cowering away from the army as they marched through. Some of the elves muttered amongst themselves, whilst others screamed "they're going to attack us!"

"Don't make eye contact with anyone," said Lewis. "Don't talk to anyone, either."

The army silently agreed with Lewis, and they continued their march through the village, ignoring everyone around them. Then, an elf approached them.

"Can we help you?" he asked.

"I'm sorry?" said Caleb.

Behind him, Caleb could hear the army grumble.

"Who are you and why are you here?" the elf questioned.

Caleb tensed for a second. Should he answer or ignore him?

"I'm waiting..."

Caleb decided to ignore the elf and continued to march on. The rest of the army followed him.

THE KING'S ARMY

"You're a stupid dick," said Jesse.

"What?" spat Caleb. "Why?"

"We said don't talk to them. And what did you do? You spoke to them!"

Caleb rolled his eyes, not responding to Jesse's comment. He continued to march forwards, this time telling himself not to interact with any of the elves of the Ice Kingdom.

As the villagers scrambled away, whimpering, and screaming, Caleb struggled to keep a straight face — the hysterics of the Ice Kingdom made him want to laugh. As if they'd attack the innocent elves — elves that had nothing to do with the abduction of Princess Kate. In the distance, Caleb could see more mountains, lined up across the landscape with snow settled along the rock.

"I think we're almost out of here," said Jesse. "Let's just keep going."

Ahead of them, warriors and wolves appeared. The villagers screamed manically, running into buildings to get to safety.

"You're *not* going to get to the princess!" yelled one of the warriors.

"Lads, get ready!" Jesse screamed. "Attack!"

The King's Army charged towards the warriors of the Ice Kingdom. The warriors fought back, the wolves shooting through the village, their paws pounding against the ground. Caleb positioned his bow and arrow, shooting multiple arrows at the enemy. Only two of them hit their targets. Caleb fumbled with his belt to grab another arrow. He couldn't feel any.

THE KING'S ARMY

Looking down, Caleb cursed as he realised that he had no arrows left.

"Use your sword," said Lewis.

Caleb drew his sword and sliced a wolf's ear, the wolf screaming out in pain and collapsed to the floor. It tried to get back up, but the loss of blood was making it weak. Its energy soon ran out and Caleb watched the wretched beast die a gruesome death.

Caleb ran towards the other warriors and swung his sword at one of them, attempting to knock them down. But he missed, sending himself flying. The warriors all charged towards him and his fellow army troops, unleashing a vicious attack.

"Attack!" Jesse shrieked.

The King's Army wielded their weapons once again, the sound of swords clashing together ringing in Caleb's ears. He saw one of the warriors charge towards him and swung his sword in defence. He caught the man's neck, drawing a nasty gash. A deep wound formed, and blood poured from the warrior's throat. He died instantly, tumbling to the ground with a thud.

Wolves continued to charge towards the King's Army in all directions. Caleb didn't know how he was going to survive this. Without warning, a surge of energy rumbled through the village, sending many of the wolves into walls, buildings, and barrels of sharp objects. Caleb watched as his friends used their many forms of magic to fight against the wolves. Tobias jumped into the air and slammed back down with a

THE KING'S ARMY

heavy force, pummelling a wolf's head into the ground, snapping its neck.

"Look out!" Caleb yelled.

Above, a dragon shot down, flapping its wings violently, preparing to send everyone in the King's Army in numerous directions across the village. Jesse got his crossbow ready and lit one of the arrows tips on fire with a torch hanging from one of the buildings. He aimed it straight towards the dragon's neck, setting it alight and sending it flying around in the air in a frantic, panicked mess, before pummelling to the ground and burning to death.

"Nice shot," said Caleb.

He swung round and punched a warrior in the face, sending him flying backwards, blood shooting from his nose. The warrior growled and charged towards Caleb. He rubbed his hands together and pushed them on Caleb's chest, sending a violent pain through Caleb's skin and straight to his heart. Caleb collapsed to the ground, gasping for air. He couldn't breathe. His heart was in severe pain.

"Help," Caleb spluttered.

It felt like he was having a heart attack.

The army couldn't do much to help him—there were still so many wolves, dragons, and warriors to fight against. Caleb clutched his chest, trying to steady his breathing. Was this the end?

Henry raced over to him and dragged him round the back of a building. He tore Caleb's clothes from his torso and studied his muscular chest. A black, burning

THE KING'S ARMY

wound sat in the centre of Caleb's chest, just about exposing his heart. Caleb shivered as a tall, wide figure towered over him and Henry.

"I'm not done with you," the figure growled.

Henry stood up and punched the elf in the gut, before giving him a second blow to the face. He drew his sword and sliced it across the attacker's chest, tracing a long, deep wound through his flesh. Caleb watched but was struggling to keep awake. His injuries were making him pass out.

Henry turned back to Caleb and crouched down next to him. Caleb took in deep breaths, but his eyes were beginning to close, the world slowly drifting away.

"Oh, shit," whispered Henry. "Where's this healer?"

Caleb's eyelids flickered as he continued to try to stay conscious. "Matilda?" He just about managed to say her name. He wanted her. The desire to see her one last time was strong. "Please get her."

Henry looked around. He didn't know what to do or where to find her. "Where is she? I don't know where she is."

"I'm here," a gentle voice said.

Caleb smiled as Matilda made her way round to him. She looked even more beautiful than she did before. The healer asked Henry to move, and she crouched down next to Caleb. He tried to lift his arm to reach out to touch her face. But he couldn't—he was too weak.

THE KING'S ARMY

"Help me," said Caleb.

"I'll try my best," said Matilda. "Your injury is quite severe, and it won't be easy to heal."

"Please. Try."

Matilda nodded and studied Caleb's wound for a few minutes. Time was running out and he was so desperate for her to save his life. If he died, he wouldn't be able to fight for her. She was all he wanted. He no longer cared about Princess Kate.

༄

Caleb regained consciousness, but everything around him was a blur. He didn't know where he was or who he was with. All he knew was that he was alive, and that was all that mattered to him. He closed his eyes and opened them again, hoping his vision would be clearer. It was still a blur, but he managed to make out some objects.

A sword.

A barrel.

Painted portraits.

A dressing table.

Soon, his surroundings came into focus. Caleb still didn't know where he was. He felt a soft, fluffy mattress underneath him. Looking to his left, he spotted a familiar face. A familiar, *beautiful* face.

Matilda.

"Where am I?" Caleb asked.

THE KING'S ARMY

"Oh, you're awake," Matilda said. "Welcome back."

Caleb smiled. "Where am I?"

"You're in the palace." Matilda stood up and leaned over him, checking his pupils and studying his wound, making sure it had fully healed. "I had to sneak you in. Nobody knows you're here."

Caleb tried to speak but no words came out. Was he pleased or was he disappointed? He didn't want to be stuck in the palace, he wanted to be out fighting.

"Where are the others?" Caleb asked.

"They're still out," replied Matilda. "I only brought you back here because of how badly injured you were. But you may as well stay now."

"I can't. I need to find the princess."

Matilda frowned. "I thought you didn't care about her."

"I don't. But I care about my mother and my sister. I'm doing this for them."

"But if you save her and marry her, what happens with us?"

Caleb didn't really know what to say. Right now, there wasn't an 'us' with him and Matilda. They weren't in a relationship; heck, they barely *knew* each other. He didn't want to get Matilda's hopes up about a future together, no matter how much he felt for her.

"I don't know," said Caleb. "I have to marry her, so my family have a home. That doesn't mean I have to *love* her."

"Love?" Matilda winked, a shy smile on her face.

THE KING'S ARMY

"Yeah, I don't have to love the princess. I just have to marry her - and stay married to her."

"I thought you meant— never mind."

Caleb was confused. He sat up with a struggle and stroked Matilda's hand. "No, go on. What did you think?"

Matilda sighed. "I thought you meant you didn't have to love the princess because you loved *me*."

Caleb pulled his hand away and giggled nervously. "Oh."

"Well, do you?"

"I—"

"Take that as a no."

"I didn't say that. I'm just a bit shocked, that's all. We barely know each other and have only been *together* once. I can't love you *yet*."

Matilda got up and wandered over to her dressing table. She picked up a scalpel made from wood and carried it over to Caleb.

"What's that?" Caleb asked, worried.

"I need to take the bandage off your wound. I can't just pull it off."

She brought the scalpel down to where the bandage was sealed and sliced it down the seal. Caleb let out a sigh of relief. He couldn't believe he had been stupid and thought Matilda was going to hurt him.

"Are you okay?" Matilda asked.

"Yeah," said Caleb with a light chuckle. "Sorry, I thought you were going to stab me or something."

THE KING'S ARMY

Matilda giggled. "I'd never do that. I'm a healer, not a killer."

Caleb knew Matilda would never hurt him. He was just paranoid.

He looked around, taking in his surroundings. The room looked newly decorated with lilac walls and a golden chandelier hanging from the ceiling. Painted portraits of past heirs to the throne hung along the edges of the walls.

"Why are these portraits in your room?" Caleb asked.

"What do you mean?" Matilda asked.

"Why aren't the portraits in a corridor for all to see?"

"The queen doesn't like to look at past kings and queens. She only cares about herself. And I, being her least worthy member of the palace, have to have all her shit in my bedroom."

"It's not fair. You heal all of us injured elves; you should be one of her *most* worthy members."

Caleb climbed off the bed and wandered around the room. He had never been in a woman's bedroom before so he didn't know what he would expect to find.

"Bed is comfy," said Caleb.

"Indeed, it is," replied Matilda.

She turned to face him and smiled. Caleb stared at her lips. God, he just wanted to kiss her—again. His eyes were drawn from her lips to her eyes. But they were dragged downwards to her breasts. He didn't take his eyes off them, he was drawn in. Everything about

THE KING'S ARMY

this woman was amazing, and Caleb didn't want anything or anyone except *her*.

"Did I say you could look?" Matilda teased.

"Sorry," said Caleb, taking his eyes off and looking at her face again.

"I'm joking. You can look all you want." Matilda stepped closer and reached her hand out to his chest.

"And if you're lucky, you can *touch* all you want too."

Caleb's heart began to beat faster, sweat dripping down his face. He pulled her in closer and kissed her.

⚜

"I need to go," said Caleb.

Matilda stared at him. "Leave the others to it. You'll be much safer here with me."

"I need to go and do my job. I'm sorry."

Caleb scrambled out of the bed and gathered his clothes, dressing his naked body. Matilda watched him, a smirk crawling across her face.

"What are you smirking at?" Caleb said with a giggle.

"You."

"Why?"

Matilda didn't say anything. Caleb looked down and laughed. But his smile was soon wiped from his face when he heard voices outside the room.

"Shit," whispered Matilda, "hide."

THE KING'S ARMY

Caleb froze, not sure where to go. He looked at Matilda for guidance.

"Under the bed!"

Caleb jumped to the floor and crawled under the bed, making sure every part of him was hidden. He heard the door burst open and a murmur of female voices filled the room. The door closed and the voices stopped. For a few moments, the room was silent before one of the voices broke it.

"I hear you've been healing the invaders," said one of the women.

"Yeah, I have," Matilda replied. "That's my job as a *healer*."

"Oh, leave off. You don't heal the enemy, that's rule number *one*."

"They're not enemies—not really. They're here to save what is theirs. The princess doesn't belong to our kingdom, you know this."

Matilda's voice sounded quivery, and Caleb didn't like to hear this fear in her.

"Her Majesty specifically said we're *not* to get involved with the enemy, no matter what it's for. You've broken her law. You *will* be punished."

Caleb clenched his fists until his knuckles turned white. He couldn't believe the way these girls were talking to Matilda. She had done nothing wrong. All she had done was save his life.

"How will I be punished?" Matilda asked.

Caleb watched the mattress bounce above him, Matilda's legs dangling at the end of the bed. He was

THE KING'S ARMY

dreading what the response to Matilda's question was going to be. Would she be imprisoned? Killed?

"Queen Saphielle would like to see you in her court in half an hour," said another voice. "Don't be late."

The door slammed shut and the room fell silent again, except for the faint whimpering from Matilda. Caleb rolled out from under the bed and sat next to her, pulling her in close and comforting her. He closed his eyes. Her skin against his felt like nothing he had ever felt before. It was beautiful. *She* was beautiful.

"Why is the queen such a bitch?" Caleb asked.

"She hates all of us. If we aren't fighters or we don't provide much use to her, she speaks to us like we're nothing. She *treats* us like we're nothing. I'm nothing." Matilda cried even harder, squeezing Caleb tightly as she took in his comfort.

"You're not 'nothing'. You're everything. And even if you're not everything to that bitch, you are to *me*."

Matilda looked up and kissed Caleb on the lips. All Caleb wanted to do was be with her. He wanted to protect her and keep her safe. And now he was worried he wouldn't be able to do that. What if the queen's punishment was to kill her?

16

CALEB PACED AROUND the room anxiously. Matilda had left ten minutes ago to face the Winter Queen, leaving him alone in the room. He knew he couldn't leave either—that would be a death wish. Instead, Caleb had to just stay where he was and wait. What he was waiting for was something he didn't know. Was he waiting for Matilda to return? Was he waiting to hear Matilda had been decapitated? Caleb didn't know. But what he *did* know, was that he was *scared*.

A hum of voices came from outside the room. Caleb rolled under the bed, making sure he was hidden, just in case they came in. And they did.

Caleb stayed as quiet as he could. The door closed quietly, and all Caleb could see was two pairs of feet—gruesome feet. Their toes were wrinkled with overgrown nails, dirt sprinkled all over like fairy dust. He gagged as he listened carefully to what they were saying, looking away from their feet.

"Where does she keep her potions?" asked one of the voices.

"I don't know," said the other, "she keeps them very well hidden. Look in all the drawers, all the cupboards, and in *every* corner."

"Why every corner?"

THE KING'S ARMY
"It's just a saying."

Caleb heard a huff, and watched as the feet trudged across the carpet, searching for Matilda's healing potions.

"The stupid bitch made a *huge* mistake helping the enemy," said one of the elves.

"Well, the queen has dealt with her. She certainly won't be making any more mistakes like that, that's for sure," responded the other.

Caleb held in his fury. Matilda didn't deserve any of this. And what did they mean by "won't be making any more mistakes?" Had Queen Saphielle killed her? Caleb anxiously awaited more from these two arseholes.

"Found one."

Caleb couldn't hold it in anymore. He rolled out from under the bed and unleashed his anger, startling the two elves.

"What the *hell* do you think you're doing?" Caleb shrieked.

The two elves swung around and stared at Caleb, drawing their swords and pointing them in his direction.

"Who are you?" one of them asked.

"None of your business. What're you doing in Matilda's bedroom? It's an invasion of privacy."

"And what are *you* doing in her room?"

Caleb didn't respond. The two elves smirked at each other, giving a knowing look towards Caleb. Caleb wanted to attack them, hurt them as much as he could.

THE KING'S ARMY

But he knew he stood no chance against them. Both elves had large, bulky builds that could easily destroy him.

"Get out," said Caleb.

"Who are you to tell us what to do?"

"I said, *get out!*"

Caleb charged towards them, but they both teleported to the other side of the room, sending Caleb crashing into Matilda's dressing table. The two elves laughed as they watched Caleb stumble to his feet.

"Hang on," said one of the elves, "you're from the Shihan Kingdom, aren't you?"

Caleb froze. He didn't know what to say. They would know he was lying if he said 'no', but he knew he would be hurt—or worse, killed—if he said 'yes'. Either way, it wouldn't end well for him.

"You are, aren't you?" the same elf asked.

"No, course I'm not. I'm Matilda's protector," lied Caleb.

The elves burst into laughter.

"No, you're not, she's a shitty healer. She doesn't *have* a protector. And even if she did, it certainly wouldn't be someone like you." The elf looked Caleb up and down, judging the appearance of Caleb's body.

"You two are such dicks!" Caleb fumed. "Why are you all like this? Matilda has done *nothing* wrong!"

"She's helped you! That is against the Winter Queen's law. She broke that law, and now you're *both* going to face the consequences."

THE KING'S ARMY

Caleb darted towards the door and fumbled with the handle, trying to open it to escape the room. Both elves teleported next to him and grabbed him, pulling him away from the door and throwing him on the floor.

"Nice try," said one of the elves, "but you're forgetting - we're stronger than you."

"Get out of my way!" growled Caleb, getting himself steady on his feet.

He dashed towards them, but they teleported once again, sending him crashing into the door. Caleb grabbed the handle, pulled the door open, and ran down the long corridor, racing past the dozen guards who marched cautiously around the palace. He skidded to a halt and looked behind him. The guards were racing towards him. Again, Caleb ran. He turned left, taking himself down a shorter corridor, with just a few doors on either side.

A pillar.

Caleb ran to the pillar and hid behind it, staying as still and as quiet as he could. He heard the guards run straight past the corridor, continuing down the long one. Caleb poked his head around the pillar to make sure he was safe to move. And then, he made his move. He opened the door to his left and closed it gently behind him.

It was dark and Caleb didn't know where he was. There were no windows — or if there was, they were blacked out — and there didn't seem to be any sign of torches or candles. Caleb would have to find his way

THE KING'S ARMY

around in the darkness, making sure he didn't make his presence known. He had no idea what could be in this room—if anything.

He crept around, tiptoeing, carefully placing his feet on the ground after each step. The entire room could be booby-trapped. Caleb took a step forward and stepped on something squishy. It had a bumpy texture and was quite hard. He stepped down harder, awakening the beast he had just stepped on.

A pair of eyes lit up an evil red, lighting up the whole room. Caleb stumbled in fear as the dragon rose in the air, spreading its wings against the walls. Caleb screamed and ran towards the door. The room became a funnel of noise as the dragon growled, its bones cracking, and fire spitting from its mouth. Caleb grabbed the door handle, and ran out of the room, slamming the door behind him. The bang echoed around the palace.

Shit.

The door started to rattle, the dragon smashing against it from the other side. Caleb ran, hiding behind a pillar or wall every time he saw someone. Anxiety riddled within him. He just wanted to see Matilda—he just wanted to make sure she was okay. But he had this funny feeling that this morning was the last time he was ever going to see her.

"Hey!" a voice yelled.

Caleb gasped, startled by the loud tone, and ran. Arrows flew past him, just missing each area the guards were aiming for.

"Hey, stop!" the voice yelled again.

THE KING'S ARMY

Caleb didn't stop; he kept running. Approaching a staircase, Caleb stopped with a stumble. He knew if he ran down the stairs, he would probably slip and fall.

"Don't move!" the guard yelled.

Caleb jumped onto the banister and slid down it, all the way to the bottom of the staircase. The guards ran down the stairs and followed him. As he approached the front doors, he yelled with relief.

Slam.

Caleb was horrified when the doors slammed shut in front of him.

Click.

He was locked in. Now, Caleb knew he was in danger. There was nowhere for him to run—he was surrounded by guards and wolves.

"Please," said Caleb. "Don't hurt me."

The guards stood with their weapons pointed at Caleb. They showed no sign of lowering them. Caleb knew he would have to plead with them. He'd have to plead and plead until they listened and left him alone.

Ha, fat chance of that happening. They'll kill me before I can say another word.

"Who are you and why are you in here?" a red-haired elf asked.

"I'm Caleb. I was brought here to be healed." Caleb didn't really know what else to say. After all, that *was* the reason Matilda brought him here.

"Why would you be brought here? The healer has a place of work for a reason."

THE KING'S ARMY

Caleb shrugged his shoulders. "I don't know. She brought me here whilst I was unconscious. I have no recollection of the events."

"Where you from, boy?" another elf growled.

Caleb didn't like the look of this one; he scared him. The guard had a big bushy beard, black teeth, a large build with a hairy belly. It made Caleb want to vomit. He glared at the elf's hands - black with filth, dirty fingernails, and wounded skin. Where had this guy been, and what had happened to him?

"I—" Caleb stopped. He didn't want them to know where he was from. But he didn't want them to figure out he was lying. He sighed. "I'm from nowhere. I just travel around. No family, no friends, no home. I travel, see where I end up, and explore."

The hairy elf grunted. Caleb could see the disbelief in his eyes. He knew he had been busted. The elf grunted again before lowering his weapon.

"You must be hungry," he said, his voice suddenly soft and gentle - almost *caring*.

Caleb didn't know what to say. "I am a little bit. Haven't had a proper meal in weeks." On the inside, Caleb was smiling. Did these guards really believe him? If so, he could take advantage of this. He could get inside information, find the princess, save her, and give his family a good home.

The rest of the guards lowered their weapons and escorted Caleb up the staircase, forming a protective box around him. The wolves left and wandered off

THE KING'S ARMY

in another direction, back to their kennels Caleb presumed.

"So, where did you last end up on your travels?" a blonde-haired elf asked.

"I don't really know," said Caleb. "Just some village with huts. There wasn't much there. Must be in poverty."

Caleb couldn't handle any more questions. It wouldn't be long before he let something slip. They would know who he really was and where he came from. The elf behind Caleb shoved him, sending him plummeting to the ground.

"You think we're stupid?" he roared, pointing his sword at Caleb's neck. "We know where you're from, you lying shit!"

Caleb swallowed a lump in his throat. He was too scared to move—it could be the last move he ever made. Instead, he decided to play dumb.

"If you know where I'm from then I'd love to know because it would be great to find my family," said Caleb, smirking.

The sword edged closer. "*Don't* try to be a smart-arse. You're one of *them* - you're from the Shihan Kingdom. And we know *why* you're here."

"May as well let me get on with it then."

Caleb knew he was witty and could fight with words. But right now, he wished he had magic. Because that would be very helpful in this situation. Suddenly, a heavy bomb of energy knocked the elves through the air and hit the ground like a game of ten-pin bowling.

THE KING'S ARMY

Caleb let out a sigh of relief and scrambled to his feet. The elves were in a heap on the floor, groaning in agony. Caleb looked behind him and saw his fellow army squad marching towards him. He smiled as they approached him.

"Thanks for saving my bacon," he said.

"No worries," said Jesse. "We look after our own."

"I don't understand how we're all still alive to be honest. Especially me."

Lewis smiled. "We're not stupid, that's why. We know how to fight, and we don't play dirty."

"I just wish Shayne was here." Caleb frowned. "He would know what to say and what to do."

Damien rested his hand on Caleb's shoulder. "Don't worry, we'll get through this. We're in the palace now and one step closer to finding the princess."

"But this is where things get competitive for *us*," said Caleb. "Only one of us can save the princess."

"And we all have different reasons for doing so," said Henry. "I only want to save her so I can get some good bedroom action."

"Henry, be quiet," said Caleb. "Some of us have *real* reasons for wanting to be the one to save her."

"Like what?"

"I need to provide for my family. My mother and sister need a home and so do I. The only way I can guarantee that is by saving Princess Kate and marrying her."

THE KING'S ARMY

The army fell silent. Had Caleb got through to them? Were they finally realising there were real reasons behind saving the princess?

"May the best man win," said Jesse.

"What?" Caleb snapped.

Jesse ran up the stairs and disappeared along the corridor. Caleb had no words. Had Jesse just betrayed the entire army?

"We need to go too," said Caleb. "These guards could wake up at any moment. Let's run."

The army raced up the stairs and darted in opposite directions. Caleb, Lewis, and Damien turned left and raced along the corridor, not caring that the sun was shining brightly through the stained-glass windows, blinding them.

"Where would she be?" Caleb asked.

"She could be anywhere," said Lewis, "we just have to look in every room we come across."

"Us three need to stick together. We shouldn't do this alone."

"What about the benefits of saving her?" Damien questioned. "Like you said, only one of us can save her."

"As soon as we find her, that's when we battle it out."

The three shook hands, striking a deal. Caleb *had* to win that battle. But first, he had to find the princess.

17

AS THE ARMY charged along a corridor that ran for miles, the floor began to get slippery, disrupting Caleb's balance. He wobbled but managed to keep himself upright. *Is this leading to the Queen's private area?* "I think we should start to be more cautious here," whispered Caleb. "Queen Saphielle could live in this part of the palace and that's why it's becoming icy."

"What exactly is she going to do?" Lewis said with a laugh.

"She's a royal, the most powerful elf in this kingdom. Her magic is unbelievable. That's what Matilda said."

Damien rolled his eyes. "You believe *everything* Matilda says? Has it ever occurred to you that she might be on the queen's side? She lives here for crying out loud!"

"Don't get shitty; Matilda is a lovely, beautiful woman. She would never lie to me."

Ahead of him stood a slim, blonde-haired woman. She was dressed in a scruffy dress, her mascara running down her face.

"Matilda!" Caleb yelled.

The woman looked over at him, a blank expression on her face. Then, she ran. Caleb gave chase, trying

THE KING'S ARMY

his best to catch up with her. But he wasn't built for running on ice and he kept slipping and sliding all over the place.

"Matilda, stop!"

His voice echoed around the palace, so he decided to stop yelling. Any moment, a guard could catch him, arrest him, and kill him. He needed to stay calm and stay quiet. Matilda slowed down and came to a stop. She leaned on a banister and caught her breath. Caleb finally caught up with her and stood in her path.

"What happened?" he asked. "Are you okay?"

Matilda didn't say anything. She tried to get around Caleb, but he moved out to block her escape.

"Move," she said.

"Matilda—"

"I said, *move!*"

Matilda lifted Caleb high in the air and launched him over the edge of the banister, sending him plummeting to the ground.

Everything went black.

❈

It was all a blur. Caleb couldn't quite make out where he was as he drifted in and out of consciousness. Then, it all came into focus. He was back in Matilda's room.

"Oh good, you're awake," said Matilda.

"What…what happened?" Caleb asked.

Matilda shied away, a guilty look on her face. "I'm sorry, it was my fault."

THE KING'S ARMY

"What was your fault?"

"I...I threw you off the balcony."

Caleb sat up, angrily. "What? Why?!" Pain shot up through his spine, and he immediately laid back down again, resting his back on the soft mattress.

"The Queen. She...oh, I don't want to say it." A tear ran down Matilda's face.

"What did she do? What did that *bitch* do?"

Matilda sighed. "She punished me for helping you."

"Continue, please."

"She removed my healing powers and replaced them with a curse. It means that I can only use negative magic from now on—which means I'll hurt people."

"And you decided to hurt me. Thanks."

"No, no it wasn't like that. The curse she placed upon me makes me snap at the smallest of things. She overrules everything I do. Her curse *told* me to throw you over the edge. I didn't want to."

Caleb looked away from her. He couldn't stand the sight of her right now. But even more so, he couldn't stand the queen. She was an evil cow. She needed to be stopped. Caleb rolled off the bed and held his back as pain shot through him again. He winced.

"Be careful," said Matilda. "You don't want to hurt yourself even more."

"I didn't hurt myself the last time. That was *you*!" Caleb snapped.

Matilda frowned, and Caleb's heart sank. "I'm sorry, I didn't mean to snap."

THE KING'S ARMY

"It's okay," Matilda said, forcing a smile onto her face, "I understand why you're angry with me."

"I'm not angry with you. I'm angry with Queen Saphielle."

"She's an evil bitch, I get it. But you can't go in and have it out with her. She'll kill you!"

"I'd rather die if it means I can protect you."

Matilda laughed. "How can you protect me if you're dead?"

Caleb wondered for a moment, before giggling too. "Good point. But you know what I mean."

He gathered his weapons from the floor and attached them to his uniform. Matilda jumped to her feet and stood in front of Caleb, fear in her eyes.

"Please don't go," she whispered. "I need you."

Caleb pushed Matilda's hair behind her ears and stared into her eyes. "I have to. Don't worry, I'll be okay."

Matilda shook her head. "No, you won't. The Queen's powers are strong, you won't survive out there."

Caleb pulled her close, wrapping his arms tightly around her shoulders. He kissed the top of her head. "I'll be fine, I promise. As soon as I've found the rest of the army, we'll be able to stick together."

Matilda pulled away from Caleb's grip and smiled. "Promise?"

A smile crept onto Caleb's face. "I promise."

THE KING'S ARMY

Matilda moved out of his way and Caleb walked to the door. He turned around and looked at Matilda once more, smiling. Then, he left.

The palace was quiet except for the hushed voices Caleb could hear in the room next door. He crept over to the door and pressed his ear against it, listening to the conversation happening in the room.

"We have to do something," a male voice said.

"Her powers...they're becoming weaker."

"There isn't anything we *can* do," said a female voice. "She's the queen. No one is stronger than her. I'm sorry but there is no way we can fix her."

A loud bang and a roar came from inside the room. Caleb flinched at the angry male voice.

"You *will* fix her! Those bastards from the Shihan Kingdom need to die. If Her Majesty loses her powers, we *all* lose our powers," the man roared. "Then, we're all in the shit!"

Caleb smirked. *If Her Majesty loses her powers, we all lose our powers.* Those words bounced around his mind. This was his chance. If the queen lost her powers, he would have a huge advantage over her.

Princess Kate could be saved.

꧁꧂

Caleb found the rest of the King's Army hiding in a broom cupboard. An odd choice of a hiding place, but Caleb didn't care. He had some exciting news to tell.

THE KING'S ARMY

"You'll never guess what I've just found out," he said, giddily.

"What's happened?" Lewis asked.

"I overheard a conversation upstairs. The Queen is losing her powers."

"Holy shit, no way!" Damien exclaimed.

"Yes way! And you know what else that means?"

"No."

"It means the elves of the Ice Kingdom will also lose their powers."

The army spoke amongst themselves, excited by this revelation. This finally meant they had the upper hand. Caleb hushed them.

"So, we need a plan," said Caleb.

"What's your plan then?" Tobias asked.

"Firstly, we need to find where Queen Saphielle lives in the palace. I think I know whereabouts, but I'm not one hundred percent sure."

"And then what?" Lewis asked.

Caleb poked his head out of the door, making sure no one was listening outside. "Then, we attack. We hold the queen hostage, that's the only way she'll crack."

The army weren't sure. Caleb had been injured too much for them to believe in him. Was he really that bad at the job?

Caleb reassured them, saying everything would be okay. The queen wouldn't be able to do much, her

THE KING'S ARMY

powers were weakening so whatever she tried wouldn't last for long.

"What about Jesse?" Damien asked. "He ran off and hasn't been seen since."

"He's probably dead," said Caleb, "now come on. Let's go."

He pushed the door open slowly, making sure nobody was around. Then, the army fled, racing up the stairs and towards the icy corridor. A squad of guards marched on the other side, their swords pointing towards the ceiling. Caleb stopped the army and directed them, telling them to get ready for battle. The army posed with their weapons. And then, the guards turned the corner, marching in the army's direction.

"Guards!" the squad master yelled. "Halt!"

The squad came to a stop and stared at the King's Army, their eyes squinting. Caleb smirked.

"Army!" Caleb yelled. "Attack!"

The King's Army ran towards the squad of guards, screaming and penetrating their swords into the stomachs of the guards. Some of the guards used their powers to fight back against the army, sending them hurtling towards the banisters along the edges of the corridor—something Caleb didn't want to go through again.

Caleb circled his chosen guard, mocking his lack of ability to fight. The guard swung his sword at Caleb, but he managed to avoid it. Caleb swiped his sword at the guard's leg, producing a deep, bloody wound. The guard cried out in pain and wobbled, managing to stay

THE KING'S ARMY

upright. Caleb laughed, swiping his sword once again. The guard avoided it and sliced Caleb's arm. Caleb winced but didn't scream—he needed to be brave. He wouldn't give in to them.

A cry came from behind him, and Caleb swung around, watching Lewis fall to the floor, covered in his own blood. Two guards had attacked him, both stabbing him in the stomach and chest with their swords. Caleb turned back around and swung his sword at the elf behind him, slicing it across his neck, decapitating the bastard.

"Holy shit!" Henry cried. "Caleb!"

Caleb stumbled backwards, feeling faint. He couldn't believe what he had just done. Staring at the headless body, Caleb's stomach lurched, and his skin turned pale. Suddenly, he vomited all over the floor and the body.

The guards ran towards him and grabbed him. Caleb struggled against them, kicking, and screaming at them. Damien raced towards the guards, using his powers to knock the guards to the floor, losing their grip on Caleb.

Caleb stood up and stabbed his sword into the chest of one of the guards. He held it for a few seconds before pulling it out of the wound, the blood pouring out and the guard slowly fading away from the world. The army followed Caleb's actions, and each killed the remaining guards, listening to their screams of agony bounce off the walls. Then, they walked away like nothing had ever happened.

THE KING'S ARMY

"Are you okay?" Tobias asked. "You violently vomited back there."

"I'm all good," said Caleb, "it was just the shock of it. I'm fine now, though."

The army walked carefully along the icy corridors, icicles as long as ten inches hanging from the ceiling, frozen spikes sticking out from the banisters. As they made their way through the palace, it grew darker. There were no windows, just the faint glow of torches secured to the walls.

"I think she lives up here," whispered Caleb.

"It stinks along here," said Damien. "Are you sure the *Queen* is going to live up *here?*"

"It makes perfect sense. Hidden away from society, she can do whatever she wants."

As the army continued their trek along the corridor, Caleb spotted a set of large double doors, a golden plaque secured on the left door. He couldn't quite make out what it said so he walked faster, edging closer to the door.

COURT.

Caleb took a deep breath. "I was right, she does live up here. This is her court. Matilda was here only a few hours ago."

"Why was she here?" Henry asked.

"The Queen was punishing her for helping me. Matilda's healing powers have been removed and replaced with bad magic. That's why she launched me off that balcony."

THE KING'S ARMY

Caleb turned back to the doors, the temptation to go in growing rapidly. But he stopped himself. Who knows *what* could happen if he did go in.

"Well, now we know where her court is," said Damien, "we should be able to find her pretty easily. Her offices or whatever they are won't be too far from here, surely."

They turned left and followed the corridor down to the end, walking past the pillars stretching from the floor to the ceiling with icy spikes sticking out from them, a death trap for some.

A passageway to the right welcomed the army with open arms. Caleb made his way through it, the passageway lit up brightly with torches. The army followed closely, making as little noise as they possibly could.

Then, Caleb heard it.

A whimper. A cry.

"Hello?" he called.

The whimper came again, but it was so faint that he couldn't quite work out where it was coming from.

As quickly as they could, the army mad their way down the passageway, being careful not to make too much noise. Again, Caleb heard the whimper. Only this time, it was louder and clearer. It sounded like it was coming from the room to his left. Caleb pressed his ear against the door. Muffled voices came from inside the room.

"I think she's in here," said Caleb.

THE KING'S ARMY

He stepped away from the door and stared at it for a few moments.

THE THRONE ROOM was engraved into a golden plaque. Was this where the queen lived when she wasn't sleeping or being a bitch? Caleb wrapped his hand around the doorknob and pleaded with himself to open the door.

"Don't go in," whispered Damien, "she could be dangerous. We have to go about this carefully."

"The princess could be in here!" Caleb spat. "We have to save her."

Damien tried to respond but was cut off by Caleb opening the door. Caleb turned the doorknob and viciously pushed the door open. Inside the room stood Queen Saphielle towering over a young, slim woman. Her golden red hair was messy, and her face was make-up free. But Caleb knew who she was.

Princess Kate.

18

QUEEN SAPHIELLE GROWLED, swiping her sword from the table and stomping over to the army, swinging the sword angrily, ready to strike it at the first person she approached — and that was Caleb. A burst of energy knocked her back, sending her sword sliding across the floor. Caleb ran towards it to pick it up.

"Leave it!" the Queen screamed.

Without touching Caleb, Queen Saphielle pulled him away from the sword and pushed him against a cabinet, the glass smashing against his back. Caleb cried out in pain as the Winter Queen picked up her sword and started swinging it again. She brought it up behind her shoulder and swung it down towards Caleb. Caleb darted out the way and watched as the queen stabbed a tabletop with the sword.

"Get back here!" hissed Queen Saphielle.

Caleb pulled his sword from his back and pointed it at the queen. He couldn't believe such a…beautiful…woman could be so violent. The queen's appearance was something like Caleb hadn't seen before. She was a beast, yet she was beautiful — so beautiful. Nothing like his dream. Her silvery-white hair was tied into a tight bun on the back of her head, plaits leading from her fringe to the back. Her long, sparkly blue

THE KING'S ARMY

dress didn't once get caught on her silver heels. Caleb was in awe of this woman.

Queen Saphielle ripped her jewels from her neck and tossed them on a chair, like she didn't care for their value. She untied her bun and plaits and shook her hair like a horse shakes its mane, her long, silvery locks falling against her breasts. Caleb knew he was against a real fighter. He was screwed.

Another bomb of energy rushed towards the queen, taking her out once more. She hit the floor with a thud and didn't move for a few seconds. Caleb wondered if she was dead. He crept over to her, his sword still pointing in the direction of her chest. Without warning, she jumped up and slashed Caleb's chest with her sword, ripping his uniform and leaving a nasty gash streaking from his left nipple up to his right shoulder. Caleb winced but didn't react. He had to fight, he didn't have time to scream and cry.

"You bitch!" Caleb roared.

He lurched towards the queen and stabbed her left leg with his sword, thick, red blood instantly oozing from the wound. Queen Saphielle screeched as the attack sent pain shooting through her, but she shook it off and flew towards the army. Caleb rolled under a table, inviting the queen to attack his fellow army. Of course, he knew they'd easily be able to fight against her.

She used her powers to push the army around the room, but as time went on, her powers grew weaker. Just as she pushed Tobias against a wooden beam, her power weakened, leaving Tobias to wobble

THE KING'S ARMY

and fall to the floor, just missing the nail sticking out of the wood. Caleb crawled out from under the table and approached Princess Kate.

"Are you okay?" Caleb asked. "Did she hurt you?"

Princess Kate nodded. A cloth secured to her mouth prevented her from speaking. Caleb removed it so she could answer his question properly.

"I'm okay," said the princess, "but I am a little hurt. I don't want you to look though, I want a woman." She tried to move, but she didn't get far. A chain tied to her leg prevented her from getting up.

"I know *just* the person," said Caleb.

He stood up and sneaked out of the room whilst the others were distracting the queen. Matilda was the only person who could help Princess Kate. He knew that she no longer had healing powers, but she had experience in first aid so he was certain that Matilda would be able to reduce the princess' injuries — at least for a short while.

Caleb hurtled through the passageway, being careful not to trip over. As soon as he left the passageway, he was plunged into darkness. The torches along the walls had been extinguished, leaving Caleb to make decisions based on what he could remember when he was in this corridor earlier. He closed his eyes, trying to imagine what the corridor looked like, and gathered his coordinates. Then, Caleb walked on. He took small steps, sometimes taking a large step over an object he

THE KING'S ARMY

thought was there. Of course, he didn't know for sure if there was anything there or not.

The palace was silent once again. Sweat dripped down Caleb's forehead and he drew his sword from his back, pointing it outwards in front of him, just in case he needed to use it. Matilda's room felt like it was miles away despite it being along the next corridor. Caleb trudged through the corridor and leapt behind a pillar when he spotted a couple of guards marching in his direction. His heart was beating profusely, hammering against his chest. Sweat continued to drip down his forehead like raindrops on a window. He tried to control his breathing, making sure to stay as quiet as possible. If he got caught, it would all be over.

"If we find any of those elves from the Shihan Kingdom, they're dead," said one of the guards.

Caleb closed his eyes so that he didn't have to watch them walk past him. He thought if he couldn't see them, then they wouldn't be able to see him.

"Keep your eyes peeled," the other guard responded, "they could be anywhere. That king of theirs has a lot to answer for."

Caleb furrowed his brow. What did they mean, *the king has a lot to answer for?*

Caleb didn't move until it went silent, and he was certain the guards had disappeared. Now he was in a part of the palace that had light seeping through the windows, Caleb found it a lot easier to navigate his way back to Matilda's room.

"Hey!" a voice yelled.

THE KING'S ARMY

Caleb swung around and spotted a guard ahead of him.

"Shit," said Caleb.

He bolted in the opposite direction of the guard and didn't stop. He turned every corner he could see, despite them leading him in the wrong direction. The sound of heavy footsteps echoed around him, and he knew the guard was getting closer. Now was *not* the time to get caught.

A gentle breeze brushed past Caleb, sending a chill through his body. The corridor seemed empty, and Caleb sighed with relief, leaning against a wall. He wouldn't stop for long; he just needed a few minutes to catch his breath.

"You're a trespassing bastard!" a voice spat.

Caleb looked around but nobody was there. *It's just in my imagination.*

Just as he started to walk away, he was pulled back and slammed against a wall, a shot of pain firing up his spine. "What the —"

The guard appeared from behind a shield of invisibility. "You're dead."

Caleb swallowed a lump in his throat as fear rippled through him. "Pretty sure I'm still alive." He tried to hide his smirk, impressed with his quick-witted comeback.

"Don't be a smart-arse," hissed the guard. "You shouldn't be here."

THE KING'S ARMY

"Shouldn't I? Okay, I'll go then." Caleb began to walk away but was pulled back again and pinned against the wall, this time the guard not letting go.

"There is only *one* way out for you—death!"

Caleb laughed in the guard's face, an attempt to hide his fear and to humiliate the guard. But he could see that it wasn't working, and his smile soon turned to a frown. As the guard stared at him directly in the eyes, Caleb thought of a plan to escape. It took him a moment to figure it out, but he had finally settled on a plan.

"Okay," said Caleb, "here's the deal. You let me go, and I promise to leave."

The guard scoffed. "A likely story."

"You don't believe me? Okay." Caleb lifted his knee and pounded it into the guard's crotch, sending him stumbling backwards and collapsing to the floor, dropping his weapons. The guard groaned in pain, holding his crotch. Caleb swiped the shield that the guard had dropped and ran off with it. He studied it as he ran, and spotted a small diagram etched into the back, symbolising a hand rubbing the shield in one circular motion. Curious, Caleb copied the action and instantly became hidden from the world, and he raced through the palace, heading to Matilda's room.

He knocked on the door and waited for it to open. A few moments later, the door swung open, and he was greeted by Matilda. At first, Matilda was confused and began to close the door, but then Caleb removed the shield and became a visible figure again.

"How did you—" Matilda began.

THE KING'S ARMY

Caleb cut in. "No time to explain. I need you to come to the Throne Room *now*. The princess is in trouble and needs *your* help."

"My help?" Matilda questioned.

"Yes, *your* help. Come, quick!"

Caleb headed back to the door and beckoned for Matilda to follow. But she didn't.

"Are you coming?" asked Caleb.

Matilda didn't answer.

"Matilda?"

"I'm sorry, I can't," Matilda finally replied. "There are reasons why I can't, not to mention I can't do any healing if that's what she needs."

"All she needs is a bit of medical attention," explained Caleb, "surely you can do that?"

Matilda shook her head. "I'm sorry, it's all a bit too much. It's complicated."

Caleb laughed. "How can it be complicated? All you have to do is—"

"I don't mean the medical side of it. I mean the...the *personal* side of it."

Caleb didn't have a clue what Matilda was talking about, but he didn't have time for any of it. He needed her help—the *princess* needed her help.

"Can't you just put your personal life to the side for *ten* minutes and help save a life?" Caleb asked, desperate for Matilda to follow him.

"I can't," said Matilda, "I'm sorry."

Caleb scoffed and shook his head. "I don't know what I *ever* saw in you. You're selfish, you're cruel!

THE KING'S ARMY

Then again, it's no wonder considering you live in the same palace as the Winter Queen."

Matilda held back her tears. Despite this, her eyes were still bloodshot.

"Don't start with the tears."

"I'm sorry," Matilda whimpered. "You don't understand."

"Oh, I understand *perfectly*. You're too selfish to help save another life because you're too busy feeling sorry for yourself," spat Caleb. "You know what? Forget it."

Caleb turned to leave the room, anger raging within him. He gathered himself and then left the room. A hand grabbed his shoulder and pulled him back inside.

"What are you doing?" Caleb screamed.

"I need to explain," said Matilda. "We can't leave it like this."

"Go on then. Explain."

Matilda gestured for Caleb to sit down next to her on the bed. She turned towards him and took hold of his hands. Caleb tried to pull away, but Matilda's grip was too strong for him.

"The reason I can't go in that room is because of the Queen," said Matilda. "The way she's treated me, the way she talks to me. It's too much."

"Is that it?" Caleb scoffed.

"No, there is more. The Queen has a terribly dark secret that only those closest to her know. I'm not

THE KING'S ARMY

supposed to know, but I overheard a meeting between her and her staff when they were planning the abduction."

Matilda looked away from Caleb, shying away from telling the rest of the story. Caleb relaxed, almost showing sympathy towards her. It was obvious she was hurting.

"Can you tell me?" Caleb asked, softly.

Matilda shook her head. "I shouldn't. Even I'm not supposed to know, let alone someone from a completely different kingdom."

"I won't tell anyone. I promise."

Matilda took a deep breath and looked Caleb in the eyes. "She's Princess Kate's real mother."

It felt like everything had come to a stop. Caleb's mind swam with questions. How could Queen Saphielle be the princess' mother? Was the king in on this the whole time? Caleb didn't quite believe it, but at the same time, it made sense. *That* would be why the queen kidnapped the princess.

"Are you sure?" Caleb asked.

Matilda nodded. "Yes. When the Queen was first planning to abduct the princess, she told her staff that she wanted her daughter home."

"But why are you so upset about this?" Caleb was confused. "How does this affect *you*?"

A tear trickled down Matilda's face. Caleb wiped it away with his thumb and rubbed her cheek to calm her down. He smiled at her, comfortingly.

THE KING'S ARMY

"Because...because I'm *also* her daughter," said Matilda.

"Holy shit." Caleb was in disbelief. This whole time he was having it away with the Winter Queen's daughter and he didn't know? There was nothing about her that gave him even the *slightest* hint.

"I'm sorry for lying to you," Matilda muttered. "I just didn't want you to think less of me. I'm nothing like her, I promise."

Caleb forced a smile onto his face. "I know you're not. But I can't have anything to do with you, not like this anyway."

"Why not? We can run away. We can...we can start a whole new life together."

"Matilda, stop."

"Please, Caleb! I need you."

Caleb shook his head. "I'm sorry, but it just isn't possible. You're related to one of the worst beings in this world. I know you're nothing like her, but she's placed a curse upon you. You've already struck out at me once because of it and I'm scared it could happen again."

"Yet you came back here to see me."

"Only because I know you're good at what you do. Someone needs your help. Please Matilda, the princess needs you."

Matilda sighed. "I understand that you don't want anything to do with me after finding out the truth. But what I *don't* understand is how you can *judge* me for not being what you expected. You've spent your entire

THE KING'S ARMY

life being judged for who you are, yet you judge *me* because of who my mother is!"

"I'm sorry."

"You're not though, are you? Because you won't be with *me* because I've got that bitch's blood in my body. But you'll marry Kate who *also* has that bitch's blood in her body."

Caleb scoffed and stood up. He swung the door open but stopped. It suddenly occurred to him that Matilda was right. He *was* being judgemental. But he couldn't be with someone who had lied to him. Thinking about it, he didn't even want to be a part of the royal family anymore.

"Where are you going?" asked Matilda.

"To rescue the princess. She's in danger," said Caleb.

He ran out of the room before Matilda could say anything else and activated the shield of invisibility. The way back to the Throne Room was a lot quicker than it was before. As Caleb approached the passageway, he slowed down. He didn't remove the shield - he wanted to surprise the queen.

The Throne Room was just feet away from Caleb. He was so close, yet it felt like he was so far. And then, he was there. The door was already open. Caleb sneaked in but his mouth dropped, and his heart sank when he saw what was going on in front of him.

Henry—dead.

Tobias—dead.

Damien—still fighting.

THE KING'S ARMY

The room was full of wolves, dragons, and guards, all helping the queen. Damien was still going strong, his magic too much for everyone to handle. The queen tried to use her powers on him, but they were growing weaker. Caleb picked up an axe from the wall and ran over to the wolves, decapitating every single one of them.

"What the—" screamed a guard.

He looked at the bloodshed he had just caused. Dead wolves were scattered all over the floor. The queen had stopped fighting with Damien for a moment just to stare and take in what had just happened around her. She scowled and pursed her lips, confusion written all over her face.

"Who-" she began, but then stopped.

Caleb made sure not to reveal his identity. This was his advantage. He may not have magic powers himself, but he sure did manage to find a way to have magic on his side. And he wasn't about to let that go. Although, he hated the fact he could only fight with one hand - the other hand was holding the shield. If he dropped that, it would all be over for him.

"Whoever you are," the Queen shouted. "*Whatever* you are, you better come out immediately. Otherwise, you'll be in *big* trouble and the consequences won't be very nice."

Caleb giggled quietly. He knew the queen was just shooting her mouth off. What was she going to do? Her magic was getting weaker, it was just a matter of time before she was just like him - nothing.

19

CALEB PROWLED AROUND the room like a lion sneaking up on its prey, holding his sword out in front of him and stabbing the guards, one by one, until there were just two left standing. He argued with himself, one voice in his head telling him to stay hidden, the other telling him to reveal his identity and fight properly.

He looked behind him. Princess Kate was still had the heavy chain tied to her leg, her hair a soggy mess from all her sweat. She was the reason he was here. He *had* to save her. Matilda had betrayed him, now was his chance to make things right with himself for all the things he had thought and said about the princess.

Remove the shield. Reveal who you are.

Caleb fought against the temptation, but he eventually gave in. Slowly, he lowered the shield. The queen roared with anger as she realised who had just killed all her wolves and most of her guards.

"You shit!" she screamed.

Queen Saphielle raced towards Caleb, but he rose the shield, once again going invisible, and darting out of her path. He kept popping out from behind the shield, winding the queen up, and testing her patience.

THE KING'S ARMY

"Don't think you can hide forever," said the Queen, "I have dragons that can sense where someone is. Invisibility doesn't make you immune from my dragons' senses."

Caleb's voice from behind the shield was muffled. "As long as I take you down, I don't care."

"Can you repeat that? You were muffling." The Queen let out a loud, evil laugh.

"Shut up you *bitch*!"

Caleb raced towards the queen and sliced her leg with his sword, causing a slight wound up her thigh. She cried out in pain and fell to the floor. Caleb stopped and watched as she sat on the floor clutching her leg. Her makeup was dripping down her face, her hair soaked with sweat. She was a woman on the warpath and Caleb knew she wouldn't give up. Not until she was dead. Without warning, she let out a deafening whistle, and seconds later, five dragons flew into the room, knocking everything and everyone over.

"Find him," growled the Queen.

Without having to be asked twice, the dragons swooped high into the air and took in a deep breath each. Then, they darted in Caleb's direction.

Shit.

Caleb raced across the room, going round in circles again and again. He knew it wouldn't be long before the dragons caught him, and he had nowhere else to run to. But he wanted to have a bit of fun first. After all, if his time was almost up, why spend his final

THE KING'S ARMY

moments worrying about death when he could mess with the dragons' heads? He lowered the shield, revealing his face for only a few seconds before hiding again and rolling under a table, sending the dragons crashing through it and tumbling on the floor in a heap. The queen let out a frustrated scream, her face full of fury and desperation. Caleb knew she wanted to win this - but he wasn't going to let her. She was going *down*.

The dragons rose from the floor and hovered in the air for a few seconds before swooping towards Caleb. Caleb dived out of the way and picked up the sword he had dropped on the floor only minutes ago. He swung it at the dragons, clipping the claws on one of them. It let out a high-pitched squeal and hit the ground with a thud.

"No!" the Queen screamed. "You stupid shit!"

Caleb laughed and swung the axe at another dragon. He missed. Damien used his magic to hide the weapons scattered across the floor. One by one, he picked them up and launched them across the room, striking the dragons and sending them crashing to the ground or smashing through the furniture, taking their last breaths before dying. The queen screamed again and stood up, prowling through the room, trying to find Caleb.

She pointed at Damien. "You're going to pay for this."

"Am I?" Damien said, smirking.

THE KING'S ARMY

Caleb lowered the shield, showing himself for the last time. He threw the shield against the wall, shattering it into thousands of pieces. Queen Saphielle scowled and lunged at him, holding her arms out ready to grab and tackle him to the ground. Caleb jumped out of her way and sent her crashing into a jewellery cabinet. The glass shattered, and the jewellery that was worth millions fell from their hooks and shelves, hitting the floor and breaking in half.

The queen tried to use her magic. But she couldn't. Caleb smiled as he realised the queen had finally lost her powers. All the stress and the impact of her body crashing through the furniture had weakened her magic quicker than Caleb had thought it would.

"No!" cried the Queen. "My magic!"

Caleb and Damien stood over the queen and glared at her. She looked distraught, broken, finished. Her magic had gone, and she herself had weakened. Once, she was full of energy. Now, she was powerless.

"Please," Queen Saphielle whimpered, "don't kill me."

Damien picked up an axe from the wall and glared at the queen. "You're an evil bitch." He ran towards her and swung the axe at her neck. With one strike, the axe sliced through her flesh and bones, sending her skull flying across the room.

"Holy shit!" Caleb screamed, slightly gagging at the sight of the headless queen.

THE KING'S ARMY

The two elves gathered their breath but froze when they heard heavy footsteps above them. It wouldn't be long before they were caught.

"Let's go," said Damien. "You get Princess Kate, you deserve it."

Caleb tried not to smile, but deep down inside, he was over the moon that Damien had suggested this.

"Are you sure?"

"I'm sure. You got through this entire battle without using magic. Well, except for the shield that you stole but that doesn't count as it wasn't your *natural* magic. And your family need a home."

Caleb looked back at the princess, who was passed out on the floor. He didn't know if she had any idea what had happened, or if she had fainted from the sight of it all. But either way, he was happy. Happy he could return home to his family and give them the good news.

⋈

Caleb and Damien headed back towards their ship, Caleb carrying the princess tightly in his arms. In the distance, the ship glowed in the sunlight, the golden mast sparkling like treasure. They were so close to getting home.

"Caleb!" a female voice yelled.

Caleb turned around and saw Matilda dashing towards him. He turned back around and continued walking. Whatever Matilda had to say, he didn't want

THE KING'S ARMY

to hear it. She had been lying to him this whole time, something he could never forgive her for.

"You should talk to her," said Damien, "it's not her fault she launched you over that balcony."

"Trust me, you don't know the half of it," Caleb replied. "I want nothing more to do with her."

Caleb stopped suddenly when Matilda appeared in front of him, speeding past him and stopping him in his path.

"Please," she said, "just hear me out."

"No," said Caleb. "You betrayed my trust."

"And with good reason!"

"Please, just leave me alone. I'm angry you lied to me; I don't appreciate liars. Honestly, I'm okay with you being the daughter of the Winter Queen, but we can't have anything special. I don't want anything with the princess either because of her heritage, but I have no choice."

He looked down at Princess Kate, who was still stirring in her sleep. In that moment, all he could see was the Winter Queen; and for a moment, he considered leaving her in the Ice Kingdom. But then he remembered, he needed to get the princess home. His family needed that same home.

"I had to lie!" Matilda yelled. "Otherwise, you'd have come for me too!"

Caleb ignored her desperate pleas and walked around her. The ship wasn't too far from here and once he was on that ship, he wasn't turning back. He wanted to forget about this place.

THE KING'S ARMY

Matilda continued to plea with him, and Caleb kept ignoring her. He and Damien blocked out her cries and didn't once look back. They both hurried towards the ship, and just as they got to the door, a dragon flew straight towards them, picking up Damien by his head and biting down hard.

"No!" cried Caleb.

He knew he was next, and he couldn't hang around. Without having to think twice, he pounded up the steps and closed the door of the ship. He settled Princess Kate onto one of the beds and then he unanchored the ship and began to sail away.

"I'm coming home, Mum," said Caleb, looking into the distance.

20

THE SOUND OF cheers rang in Caleb's ears as he approached the ship docking station at the edge of his kingdom. His face gleamed with pride and joy as he watched his community cheer for him. But for some reason, he felt like they were expecting someone else. They'd have a nasty shock when he came out of the ship with the princess.

He threw the anchor over the edge of the ship and watched it plant itself in the sand, securing the ship in place. Taking a deep breath, Caleb walked down the steps to the lower deck and woke the princess.

"Princess," he whispered, lightly shaking her shoulder. "You need to wake up."

The princess came round and blinked a few times, confusion written on her face. "Where am I?"

Caleb smiled. "Home. You're home."

※

Screams from the elves echoed around the kingdom as the ship's door opened. Then, Caleb stepped out of the darkness and revealed himself to the kingdom, holding the princess' hand. Suddenly, the cheers stopped, and everyone muttered amongst themselves. Were they

THE KING'S ARMY

disappointed? Were they pleasantly surprised? Caleb didn't know the answer—that was until the cheers started again, ringing in his ears and his sense of pride returned. Finally, his kingdom appreciated him.

"Oh my God!" a woman screamed. "My baby!"

Caleb's eyes watered as he watched his mother push her way through the crowd and run towards him. She swung her arms around him, giving the biggest, tightest hug, she had ever given him.

"Hi, Mum," said Caleb.

Meredith pulled away and slapped Caleb. "You're a stupid, *stupid* man!" She calmed down and rubbed his arms. "But I'm proud of you. So, *so* proud. And I love you."

"I love you too, Mum." Caleb hugged his mother again. He vowed to never do anything like this again. His family was the most important thing, and he was never going to leave them again.

King Bartholomew marched over to him and held his hand out. Caleb accepted and exchanged a handshake with the king for a couple of seconds.

"Good job," said the King. "You've done well." He turned to the princess. "Hello, dear. How are you feeling?"

Princess Kate anxiously rubbed her arm. "I'm okay, just a bit shaken."

King Bartholomew wrapped his arm around her shoulders and walked with her up the stone staircase and through the village, not looking back at the man who saved her. Caleb scowled and looked into the

THE KING'S ARMY

distance. The Ice Kingdom was long out of sight, and he was glad about it. He didn't want to think about it. That place was a death trap, and his friends fell victim to it. Now that he was home, he was going to move on and start afresh. Of course, he would never forget his friends—but he sure as hell wanted to forget what he had been through this past week.

"Ladies and gentlemen!" a voice boomed. "His Highness has summoned *every one* of the Shihan Kingdom to the palace stadium. He expects you all to be there within five minutes and not a second later."

The crowd buzzed with excitement and pushed their way out of the village and over to the golden staircase that led to the Shihanian Palace. Caleb and his mother walked slowly together and found Jasmine sitting alone by the entrance to the Garden of Kate.

"Hey, sis," said Caleb, softly. "How are you?"

Jasmine looked away from him, still upset with him for leaving.

"Come on, love," Meredith said, crouching next to her daughter and wrapping her arm around her shoulders. "He's done a good thing. I'll admit I wasn't keen on the idea of him going at first. But I'm proud of him. And you should be too."

Caleb looked at his sister, anxiously. "I'm sorry, I didn't mean to upset you - both of you. But I've changed. I'm a much stronger and braver man than I ever was before."

THE KING'S ARMY

"You left us and put your life at risk," muttered Jasmine. "I was scared that the last time I'd ever see you was when you sailed away on that ship."

Caleb crouched next to Jasmine and rubbed his thumb over her knuckles. "But I'm still here, I'm alive. Come on, can we talk about this later? We've got exactly three minutes to get to the palace."

Meredith giggled. "How do you know that?"

Caleb showed her the pocket watch that he had taken from the ship. "His Highness gave this to us for our voyage. It came in handy. Now, enough questions. Come on!"

Caleb started to hurry off but stopped when he realised his mother and sister weren't following. "Aren't you coming?"

Meredith shook her head. "No. You go ahead; we'll see you later. Jasmine can't get up to the palace, so I'll stay with her."

Caleb was reluctant to go, but he knew if he didn't get up to that palace soon, he wouldn't be allowed in. So, he went.

⊰✼⊱

"Elves of the Shihan Kingdom," the King announced, "I present to you, our *champion*."

Caleb stepped out onto the stand and waved to the crowd. No one cheered for him. Still, they hated him. He stopped smiling and waited for the king to continue his speech.

THE KING'S ARMY

"He is such a brave man for doing what he did," continued the King, "and to show my gratitude, I will be blessing him."

Caleb smiled. But then, he stopped. He didn't want to be blessed with magic.

The king continued his speech. "Young Caleb will be blessed with the power of...*healing*."

Caleb choked in his own breath. Did he just hear that right?

"I've been aware of everything going on in the Ice Kingdom and how you got on so well with the healer. I forgive you for your betrayal—" he shot a scornful look at Caleb - "but after your courageous act of bravery, you deserve this. Caleb, please follow me."

The king made his way down the steps and stood in the centre of the stadium. Caleb followed and stood to attention in front of His Highness.

"Give me your hand," said the King.

Caleb held his hand out but then pulled it away. "No, wait."

Everyone in the crowd gasped and muttered amongst themselves. The king stared at Caleb, fury beginning to ignite.

"What do you mean *no*?" King Bartholomew demanded.

"I don't want to be blessed with magic. I have a different request."

The king grunted. "Explain."

"My mother and sister have stayed in the Garden of Kate. Not because they don't want to come up

THE KING'S ARMY

here, but because they *can't*. Well, my sister can't. So, instead of blessing me with magic, could you find it within your heart to heal my sister of her pain?"

King Bartholomew growled. "And what do I get out of it?"

"You get a lifetime of gratitude from myself and my family. Please, Your Highness. Once I marry your daughter, my family becomes yours too. Don't you want a family full of healthy elves?" Caleb pleaded. He was so desperate for his sister to be relieved of her pain. She didn't deserve to be in a wheelchair, she had done nothing to deserve it.

"Okay," said King Bartholomew. "Your sister can have a healthy life. On *one* condition."

"What's that?"

"You tell everyone here *exactly* what you got up to in the Ice Kingdom."

Caleb's heart dropped. If he told them he'd had an affair with the healer, they'd hate him even more than they already did. Then, he had an idea. It was risky to strike a deal with the king, but he hoped it would be worth it.

"You want me to tell them everything? So, that means I can tell them that the Winter Queen is *actually* the princess' mother and *not* your late wife?" Caleb muttered.

The king grumbled. "Well played, you win. But try anything like that again, and you *will* be punished."

Caleb smiled and turned to the crowd. Despite the joy within the crowd, Caleb couldn't help but feel

THE KING'S ARMY

like they still weren't so keen on him saving the princess. But he didn't care about that anymore.

All that mattered to him was that his sister was finally going to live a pain free life.

EPİLOGUE

"BUT I DON'T *want* to marry him!"

"Kate, you *will* marry that elf. He saved you from your iniquitous mother," said my father.

Two months ago, I was abducted from my garden, and ended up in the Ice Kingdom. I was saved by a handsome, young elf. But I don't want to marry him. I don't know *anything* about him. My father is doing exactly what my mother did—controlling me.

"Father," I said, "I don't want to be controlled by you as well. I had enough of that with Mother."

My father sighed and held my hand. "I'm sorry, I don't mean to. But do you not understand what this means? Caleb will get a home for his family, and you'll get a whole new family as well. A whole new *life*, even!"

I don't know what to do. I'm not ready to be wed, especially not to a man I don't even know. I've spent the last two months trying to get to know him, but we just don't click, and I *still* don't know him – not really, anyway.

"I'm sorry," I said. "I can't do it. I can't marry that elf."

I leave the room and hurry to my bedroom, throwing myself onto my bed and begin crying. It's a

THE KING'S ARMY

horrible situation to be in – now, I may have just made Caleb and his family homeless again.

※

Jasmine came into the room, slightly wobbling as she tried to keep her balance.

"How was physio?" Caleb asked.

"It was great," said Jasmine. "I'm getting so much better and much more confident."

"That's great, I'm so proud of you!"

There was a gentle knock on the door, before the king walked in. "Hello."

"Everything okay?" Meredith asked.

"I'm afraid not. Kate is refusing to marry Caleb. Therefore, you can't live here anymore."

"Excuse me?" Caleb roared. "How *dare* you promise us a life here, just for you to go back on your word."

The king growled. "I said, if you save her then you marry her *and* live in the palace. Not one or the other."

Meredith stormed over to King Bartholomew and stopped in front of him. She was like a dwarf compared to him, so there was no way she would intimidate him. But Meredith wanted to say her piece.

"You're a piece of shit, you know that?" she exclaimed. "We don't want to live here, anyway. Why would we?"

THE KING'S ARMY

She turned to her two children and ordered them to leave. They left the palace and wandered through the village. Once again, they were homeless.

"Why does the king hate us so much?" Jasmine cried.

"He doesn't hate us. He only hates *me*," Caleb said. "I'm so sorry."

The family were stopped by a gentle female voice. Caleb turned around and was greeted by the princess.

"What?" Caleb snapped.

"I've changed my mind," said Princess Kate. "You guys need a home. And that's only going to happen through me. So, I *will* marry you."

Caleb let a wide grin settle on his face. "Thank you. But please know that I'm not marrying you out of love. I'm doing this for my family."

"I know, I understand. After all, I *am* my mother's daughter."

Caleb chuckled. "It's not to do with who your mother is."

Kate glared at Caleb, no words necessary. Caleb backed away, uncomfortably.

"Okay, maybe a little bit."

The princess chuckled and rubbed Caleb's arm. "I'm messing with you. I'm nothing like my birth mother, but I understand you don't want to be with me out of love."

Caleb smiled, again. "Thank you, Princess."

Thank you for taking the time to read my latest work. If you have a moment, please consider leaving a review and supporting my author journey.

ABOUT THE AUTHOR

Jake Uniacke is a self-published author from Hampshire. In his spare time, he goes out and photographs the world around him, including landscapes, wildlife, and nature. Jake spent three years studying creative media at college where he found his love for photography.

As well as writing, Jake also enjoys watching films, and reading. He has always wanted to be a published author ever since he was young, and he began writing for publication in 2015. However, since then, only his most recent books are available for purchase, and the books published from 2015 to 2018 are no longer available for purchase.

Find Me:

@author_jakeu   @authorjakeu

www.authorjakeu.wordpress.com

Printed in Great Britain
by Amazon